NO DAY TO DIE . . .

Pushing the gelding through the dense willows, he concentrated on the search for dry wood until someone's strong arm swept him from the saddle. He hit the ground hard enough to jar him, and could see the attacker, dressed only in a loincloth, had his knife ready to plunge into him. Lunging, Slocum kicked him in the leg and rolled away. The knife stabbed into the ground where he'd been. Red Hawk roared like an angry grizzly, but Slocum was ready to face him.

"Today you die, white eyes!" Red Hawk charged at him, but the thick willows slowed his movements and Slocum caught his knife hand.

"Not today." Slocum twisted the arm until he had the man's hand pinned behind his back and drove him belly down on the ground.

"Let go of it!" Slocum said through his teeth and forced the knife hand higher up Red Hawk's bare back . . .

SLOCUM
AND THE LAKOTA LADY

JOVE BOOKS, NEW YORK

This is a work of fiction. Names, characters, places, and incidents are
either the product of the author's imagination or are used fictitiously,
and any resemblance to actual persons, living or dead, business
establishments, events, or locales is entirely coincidental.

SLOCUM AND THE LAKOTA LADY

A Jove Book / published by arrangement with
the author

PRINTING HISTORY
Jove edition / February 2001

The Penguin Putnam Inc. World Wide Web site address is
http://www.penguinputnam.com

ISBN: 0-515-13017-6

A JOVE BOOK®
Jove Books are published by The Berkley Publishing Group,
a division of Penguin Putnam Inc.,
375 Hudson Street, New York, New York 10014.
JOVE and the "J" design
are trademarks belonging to Penguin Putnam Inc.

PRINTED IN THE UNITED STATES OF AMERICA

10 9 8 7 6 5 4 3 2 1

1

Screaming like banshees, the three bucks came riding hell-bent for leather straight at him. Slocum barely had time to wheel the Texas cow pony around to flee when an arrow struck his right leg. It whacked hard into place like a hot knife, and he glanced down in shock to see the feathered end quivering below his knee. Several more arrows whizzed by his head. Slocum had no time for anything else but to run, and he spurred the dun horse for a coulee at a distance of fifty yards.

Cold chills from the pain shot up from his leg and caused the muscles in his jaw to tighten. Urging the pony on, he drew his Colt and without aiming, shot back at the three painted riders in pursuit of him. They veered away for some cover and distance. The dun bailed off the bank into some elder bushes, but when Slocum tried to dismount, he discovered the arrow had him pinned to the saddle's fender. He holstered the Colt, peering around, trying to locate the three warriors. Then he drew his skinning knife and began to saw the shaft between the fender leather and his pants. Already blood was soaking into his boot.

His leg free at last, he drew it over and stepped down. The weight of the waving arrow caused him more discomfort with the movement and ground deep inside his calf muscle. He tried to see the three bucks. They had drawn up at a good

distance from him in the open, and looked to be in conference
on what to do next. They were yipping and shaking their
bows in the air. Whiskey-soaked Sioux boys was all they
were.

With his right leg already too stiff to use, he managed to
drag it to the dun and jerk the .44-40 out of the scabbard. He
needed the damn arrow removed, but those three were his
main concern as he hobbled back to the chest-high bank. He
bellied down on the steep slope, loaded a round in the Winchester, and with his elbow to support the rifle, sighted in at
them.

The fattest of the three was dismounted, and dropped his
loincloth to bare his brown butt, pointing with his finger at
his rectum. It was the Indian way to taunt white men.
Apaches, Sioux, Cheyenne, they all showed off like that. A
few years earlier, during the Comanche attack on Adobe
Walls down in the panhandle country of Texas, a buffalo
hunter named Billy Dixon had given an Indian doing that a
lead enema with a .50-caliber Sharps at almost a half-mile
distance.

Slocum squeezed off the trigger, and watched the bullet
make a puff of dirt short of them. His aim was good enough.
The Sioux began to laugh at the bullet's fall: loud enough
that their hilarity carried to Slocum's ears. Another dropped
his drawers and made more offensive signs at Slocum.

Carefully Slocum aimed at the fat one, then raised the muzzle higher, being certain he had the right line. Would his
trajectory work? No way to tell. Just let it be on the mark.
Holding his breath, he squeezed off the trigger. The loud report reverberated off the grass-covered hills as smoke from
the sulphurous black powder swept by his face. Then he saw
the Indian lurch upright. His hand shot for his bare butt. Then
he was pitched forward by the impact of the bullet and
sprawled facedown.

His two companions looked on in horror at their stricken
partner. Slocum could see the one he'd shot kicking a moccasin in his pain. One thing for certain, the downed Indian
showed no sign of getting up. Never taking his eyes off his
enemies, Slocum swallowed hard against the throbbing in his

lower leg when he shifted it. With grim determination, he levered a fresh round into the chamber, leaned on his elbow, and took aim at the one on the right. With deliberate care, he raised the muzzle high enough and fired. The second Sioux was hit hard and spun around, holding his arm to his side and screaming.

That should hold those sons-a-bitches. Slocum laid down the rifle, twisted around, gritting his teeth at the pain as he lifted his wounded leg, and swung around with his back to the slope. He needed to get the arrow out. His breath was short from the exertion and pain, and he caught a few deep drafts of air. To doctor the leg, he needed some whiskey from his saddlebags. He also had a towel to use as bandage material in the saddlebags.

Slocum took a quick check of the Sioux across the way, and could see that the unharmed one, acting plenty spooked, had dragged his wounded compadres to the shade of some box elders. Not much fight left in them. He raised up to check again, and could see the young buck was either too shocked or too preoccupied to leave his dying buddies. Good, he could stay busy like that for a while.

The dun noisily grazed through his bit a few feet away. Slocum used the Winchester for a crutch, but cried out when the feathered end of the arrow struck the rifle. He paused until the waves of pain in his leg and butt eased some, then being more careful, worked his way toward the dun. Each step was hard, and when he leaned on the rifle and dragged his injured limb forward, beads of sweat ran down his face. It was a hell of a mess he'd ridden into while minding his own business.

Forced to rest, he spoke curtly to the dun to make him stand still and not move any further away. Preoccupied with filling his belly with the curly short buffalo grass, the pony clattered his teeth on the short spade bit in his mouth as he grazed. Finally, Slocum reached the horse and saddlebags. He undid the strap and threw up the flap. He drew out the bottle of McIntosh's Rye, then checked the hostiles' position. No movement. He removed the cork, and took a deep draught of the golden-colored whiskey glinting in the sunlight through the clear bottle. The whiskey would help the pain, he reminded himself, wiping his whisker-bristled mouth on the back of his hand.

Before it was over, he would have to kill that last buck out there, or the buck would kill him. Deliberately, he stripped off the silk kerchief from his neck and bent over. He used his knife to split his pants leg open below the knee on the inside. Not bothering to look at all the blood on his white skin, with grim force he shoved the arrow through his leg until a few inches of the shaft stuck through where earlier he'd sawed it off. He closed his eyes and rested. It would be lots better to sit on his butt, but he didn't trust the last Indian a hundred yards away. With his knife, he cut a groove in the shaft. The sawing on the rock-hard stem sent bolts of lightning to his brain; he fought the blinding force and braced himself with a hand on his knee. When satisfied with his notch, he knotted the end of the kerchief on the shaft's exposed end. Then, with some effort, he retrieved the whiskey bottle from the ground. With care and using his palm, he saturated the cloth in the strong-smelling rye. He set the bottle down and with both hands grasping the feathered end, tried to draw the shaft out.

With the blinding pain he was forced to quit, the arrow still unmoved. Dizzy with hurt, he sprawled on his butt. Then, with grim determination, he bent his knee back to get the arrow closer. Then, clamping his fists on the feathers, he jerked, and at last the arrow came free. Sweat rained down his face and blinded him. Lifting his leg with both hands, he managed to prop it up. When it was in place, he began to draw the whiskey-soaked kerchief back and forth through the wound. Satisfied it was the best disinfecting he could do, he used the kerchief to wrap the wound, then followed with the towel.

After fastening his crude bandage, he knew he had to get back on the dun. His only chance to survive was get the hell out of this country. Those three over there had more blood-thirsty relatives who would want revenge. And if he didn't get away soon, they'd be liable to show up.

He checked the sun. Close to noon. It was mid-June and this far north the day would be long. With an effort, he managed to half rise. Then, in a wave of hurting, he rested. He searched for a sign of that last buck, but couldn't see him.

Then he swallowed hard and rose to his feet, favoring his good leg. He swept up the whiskey and rifle. Two pain-filled steps, and then the rifle was back in the boot. He stashed the whiskey in the saddlebags. Then, using his saddle and horse for support, he studied the three paint horses. Their plaited manes were lifted by the rising south wind as they grazed off to the side.

The last Indian was moaning some kind of prayer with his friend's head in his lap. His singsong carried on the stiff breeze. For a long moment, Slocum considered scattering the three horses. That meant he had to ride up the bank of the coulee and herd them off. The notion didn't appeal to him, since he kept blinking his eyes against the raging fire in his right leg. If he couldn't run them off, he'd better shoot them. It was the only way to prevent the last buck's pursuit.

Sick to his stomach at the prospect of killing good horseflesh, he drew out the Winchester. He knew a close-by rifle shot wouldn't spook them enough. From their cropped ears, he knew they were buffalo horses and shouldn't fear the sound of guns. He spoke soothingly to the dun to make it stand steady, then laid the rifle over the seat and took the closest pony down with his first shot. The brown-faced horse threw up his head, and Slocum swung the muzzle around, took aim, and shot him between the eyes, dropping him in his tracks. At the second report, the third horse bolted away and went blistering over the rise.

Slocum swore to himself over his bad luck. The one that ran off might go back to the village and be a warning to the others. He slammed the rifle in the boot. Time for him to get the hell out of there. With some effort, he hopped on his good leg around to the side of the upset dun.

"Easy, hoss," he pleaded. With both hands on the horn, he sprang off his left leg and found the stirrup with his boot toe. Rising as high as he could and leaning over, he dragged the sore leg over the cantle and eased himself down in the seat. With some effort he bent over and put the right boot in the stirrup with his hand.

He let the pain subside some, then took one last look back

at the buck, still singing the death song for his "brothers." *Damn sure hope we never meet again, red man.* He turned the dun northward and set him in a lope. The blood in his right boot squashed around his toes.

By late afternoon, he'd avoided several Indian camps, and hoped he would soon be clear of the reservation. His wounded leg had turned to hard stone and burned like a raging forest fire, but the rye helped some to ease it. He kept under the brow of most ridges, only occasionally going to the top to check for any pursuit and make sure he didn't ride into a whole band of Indians.

The rising afternoon wind had whipped up hard. Even beneath the high points, there was little escaping the stiff breeze. Slocum wanted to stop and rest, but knew his only chance was to be off the Sioux land and in some white settlement so he could heal. He still was a long way from Montana, and questioned his judgment for cutting across the Dakotas and Sioux country to get there. Jim Lucus had written that he needed Slocum on a cattle deal in Billings.

Slocum heard a cry, and first thought it was a fox or cat. Twisting in the saddle, he searched the waving short-grass-filled hillsides, saw nothing, and decided he was going crazy from the pain and the whiskey. There he heard it again. This time, he saw the figure of a woman come over the top of the hill, stumble, and roll part of the way downhill. His hand shot to his Colt and he wondered how many rounds were left in it. He hadn't reloaded it, stupidly, with the pain and all. For emergencies, he carried a small .30-caliber Colt in his left boot. A cap-and-ball, it was good in close quarters.

He blinked at the woman. She waved to him and above the wind, he could hear her cry for help. Who was after her? Nothing else showed on the horizon. Still, he felt cautious. Was it a trap? There was not much he could tell about her. He'd seen her long braids, and she was wrapped in a colorful blanket, but there was not much else visible about her shape. She hadn't gotten up since she fell, but she waved for him to come over to her.

He shucked the empties on the ground, reloaded the Colt, then with a hard search around, felt satisfied there was no one else in sight. He pushed the dun toward her. Every few steps of the way he craned his head around to be certain she was not some kind of a bait. She lay back on her elbows, and he could see her rather striking handsome face was streaming with sweat. Her hand was bleeding, the one she'd beckoned him with. Then he saw the swell of her belly. She was very pregnant.

"Help me," she gasped, and drew her buckskin dress up to expose her shapely legs.

"Lady, I ain't a doctor," he protested, looking at her exposed genitals and the wet pubic hair plastered to her brown skin. She was fixing to have a baby. My God, what did she expect from him?

"Oh," she gasped, and lay back to strain.

He saw something black fill the widening void. *Oh, damn, she's going to have it.* How could he help? The dun snorted out his nose, and Slocum was forced to make him heel around closer. There was no way Slocum could walk to her. When he got off, he had to be there. At last, he clenched his jaws, swung his sore leg over, and dismounted, falling on the ground.

Dazed, he sat on his butt for a long moment, discovering how weak he had become. At last, he got on his hands and knees, and saw the fear in her eyes, as if she only then had realized he wasn't red, but white.

"Damnit, I'm going to try to help you," he said with effort, and dragged his injured leg, inching closer to her.

Her scream forced him to look up. Her cry wasn't over her fear of him. He could see the crown of the baby's head trying to emerge. She lay back, and he moved in between her legs in time to grasp the small slippery head as the newborn arrived in the sunlight. Raising up on his good knee, he supported the infant. She cried again, forcing the baby's shoulders out, and he moved with her efforts until the whole child was in his hands. Carefully, he wiped away the mucus from its nose and mouth with a handful of grass.

He cradled the small child in his arm, and discovered the cord was still attached to the child and her vagina. Should he cut and tie it? Something made him recall how he was suppose to slap the baby to life, so he hung it by the heels. But the slapping part was unnecessary, for the youngster began to bawl. Relieved, he smiled at the small red wrinkled thing's loud lungs and settled it in his arm.

"Cut it," she said, lying on her back and looking very pale under her copper complexion.

He set the infant on the grass, managed to draw out his knife, and separated the cord several inches from the poor thing's navel. Then he made a knot and tied it tight. She nodded her approval and held out her arms for the child. He handed the baby to her, and when he settled back with too much weight on his wounded leg, winced in pain. Then, struck in fascination, he watched her guide the babe's small round mouth to her dark nipple, shifting the long shapely teat for it to suckle. In a moment the soft sucking sounds could be heard.

Satisfied he'd done all she needed, Slocum tried to retreat by scooting back on his good knee to give her and the newborn some room. A flash of pain hit his brain and he felt himself falling forward. Tumbling into a dark abyss, he fell and fell some more into a world of darkness with nothing to catch or hold on to.

2

The hiss of the lodge poles in the grass awoke him. A small bump rocked him and made him aware that his right leg was on fire, and he reached for it. His eyes opened enough to view the azure sky; then he realized he was being moved on a travois.

Then he could hear the chatter of Indian women talking. Their laughter and good-natured voices carried above the strong breath of the day that swept up from the south. How long had he been out? It must be mid-morning. He recalled very little of the past night, nor his transfer to this conveyance.

Evidently the whole camp was moving. He could see other women dressed in buckskin leading their horses, their travois piled high with tepee skins and packs made from buffalo hides that most likely contained their food and household goods.

"You are awake?" she asked, leaning over and looking at him as she walked beside him.

He could see she carried the baby in a papoose board on her back. She swung it off her shoulder and handed it to him. "You can hold him while I find you some food."

"I can wait," he said, grinning at the little one's serious-looking face.

"Can you hold him?"

"He will be fine," Slocum said.

"I did not lose your hat either," she said, as if that was very important.

"Good," he said, his attention taken from the baby he held on his chest.

"Where do you go?" she asked with her fringed deerskin dress whipping around her long legs as she strode alongside him.

"Montana."

She wrinkled her thin nose—too narrow for a Sioux. Maybe a Cheyenne, but not a Sioux. He had known several women with such handsome faces from the Southern Cheyenne Nation in the Kansas Campaign when he'd scouted for Custer.

"It is a far way from here." She motioned with her head toward the northwest.

"I know."

"Who shot you?" she asked, never breaking her long stride to be beside him.

"Some bucks put an arrow in me. Where did you learn English?"

"Mission school."

He nodded. Had the news of his altercation with the three young bucks reached these people yet? More than likely not. All he could hope for in his condition was that those three hadn't come from this group.

"What do they call you?" she asked.

"Slocum."

She repeated it, making it two distinct syllables. "Slo-cum."

"What is your name?" he asked, nodding approval at her try.

Her guttural words were quick, and he shook his head to show he did not understand her.

"Betty Walker is what they called me at the mission."

"Betty Walker you shall be for me."

She wrinkled her nose at him as if disappointed he had not used her Sioux name. "Soon we will camp for the night."

"Good. Where are we going?" he asked, considering his

sore leg and realizing that somehow he must escape. The problem was how.

"To look for buffalo."

He agreed, and cuddled the papoose board in his arms. Somewhere in the wide procession of camp movers that were spread across the rolling grassland, two dogs jumped into a snarling fight. Quickly, a sharp-speaking squaw with a flailing quirt settled their hash, forcing them apart in yelps of protest at being whipped. Slocum knew dogs were very much a part of the Sioux life and diet. It was said that before the horse came to these people, they used dogs as beasts of burden. Now only a few carried packs, but eating their flesh remained a custom.

How bad was his leg, besides being very sore? There would be time to check it later. Then he realized that the poles he rode on were tied to his saddle and dun horse. Old Dunny had become a squaw horse whether he liked it or not. Slocum rocked the infant and tried to settle himself down. In the first place, he couldn't run away on his bad leg. Secondly, no one had acted hostile toward him, and she'd trusted him to hold her baby. Things could be a lot worse, and probably would be sooner than he liked.

They stopped to make camp near a good-sized moon lake. A body of water was trapped in a basin for lack of an outlet. It would recede as the summer sun drew out the vapors. The bull rushes around the edge were full of nesting ducks, and small ducklings swam after their parents like dutiful children. Noisy red-winged blackbirds sang from their precarious perches on the reeds that were swept around by the strong wind.

"I have a crutch for you," she said, and hurried off to get it.

Still holding the baby's papoose board in one hand, he sat up and ran the other hand down his sore leg. Man, he needed to heal up and get his strength back so he could ride on. In his present state, he couldn't handle any confrontation with that last buck if he caught up with this group. She must have taken off his holster. Luckily, he could still feel the .30-caliber in his left boot. Good place for it.

"Well, little Indian boy," he said softly, talking to the child. "You're going to see lots of changes in your life. Trust me, little fella. Trust me."

"Here," she said, and held out a stick for him with a curved piece on top to fit under his armpit.

He handed her the board, and managed to stand with her hovering close by anxious to help him. With the crutch under his arm, he found he could move and not put weight on the bad leg. It was not as good as regular crutches, but better than his rifle. He nodded in approval, and headed off for a little privacy to vent his bladder, which was about to burst.

At last, far enough away and with his back to the camp, he sought some relief. The first stream felt so good he sagged on the crutch, sending the stream off in a high arch. It was a wonder he hadn't pissed in his pants. He had begun to wonder if the flow would ever end when he heard horses. He glanced over his shoulder, and could see the men, who were obviously returning from their scout.

Finished, he buttoned his pants and hobbled back to where she'd laid out the poles to put up her tepee. The women worked in teams, standing the poles up, then pulling up the skin. An older woman bossed them, and the shelters' erection went fast. When Betty's tepee was up, she spread a buffalo robe on the ground at the entrance and told him to sit on it.

"I must help them do theirs now," she said, and left him the papoose. He watched her hurry off in a swirl of fringe around her shapely legs. Then, with care, he lowered himself to the ground and smiled at the baby. Settled at last, he drew apart the split portion of his pants and undid the bandanna. To his relief, the leg didn't look infected, but it was sore as a boil and bruised blue-black around the entrance and exit wounds, now plugged with black blood and a scab.

With nothing else to wrap it with, he redid the kerchief and bloodstained towel, then pulled down his cut pants leg. The shadow of a man fell on him and stood above him. The man's beaded moccasins looked fancy, and when Slocum raised his head and met the man's gaze, he saw the authority in the Indian's face.

"They say you are a medicine man," the Indian said. His

powerful arms were clasped over his chest, and the two eagle feathers in his braids fluttered in the wind.

Slocum shook his head. "She needed help. I stopped to help her."

"Why?"

"If you needed help, I would help you."

"But I won't have a baby."

"Baby, whatever. If you were fallen, I would see about you."

"Are you a trader?"

Slocum shook his head.

"You a preacher for the white man's God?"

"No."

"Why are you here? This is Lakota land."

"I am like the wind. I am only passing through on my way to Montana."

"How did you hurt your leg?" He motioned toward it.

"Couple of bucks out drunk and hunting thought I was a deer."

"Did they have bad eyes?"

"Damned if I know."

"What do they call you?"

"Slocum."

"My name is Kicking Dog. I believe that you are what you say you are—like the wind. For helping the woman who just lost her man and was mourning for him when her time came, you have my permission to heal your leg with us."

"I will not disappoint you."

"I know that. I can read it in your ways. We have found some buffalo today. We will celebrate tonight. You will be my guest. Some of my brothers will resent you being here. Do not take their sharp words as ungrateful for what you did for her. They have lost family to the white eyes and cannot forgive your people for it."

"I understand."

Kicking Dog nodded, turned, and strode away. Betty quickly joined Slocum with a look of apprehension written on her face.

"What did the chief say?"

"I could stay and heal in his camp."

She nodded in approval and smiled at the corners of her mouth. When she picked up the papoose, Slocum noticed she had recently amputed the end of her index finger to the first joint. The cut was open from her working with it, and bleeding.

"Go to the saddlebags and get the whiskey and white cloth," he said.

She blinked for a moment, then handed him the baby. When she returned, he made her kneel on the robe, and cleaned the raw end of her finger with whiskey on a rag. She never flinched. He wrapped the appendage in the cloth and tied it tight.

"Keep that on there so it heals," he said.

She looked at it with some apprehension, and then rushed off to help raise the other tepees. He shook his head in disapproval.

"Well, little fella, maybe it will last a few minutes on her finger," he said absently to the quiet baby.

So he was to be the chief's guest at the celebration. He wondered if the third member of the hunting party that had attacked him belonged with this group. If the young buck was a member of this band, sooner or later he would return. Kicking Dog had warned him—there would be folks who hated him for his skin color. As long as they ate their buffalo and left him alone, he didn't care. Jim Lucas's cattle deal in Montana would have to be on hold until his leg improved.

3

The Lakotas were ready to celebrate. They had a great fire going in the center of camp that licked flames ten feet high in the sky and cast an eerie orange light on the men and women in their beaded finery dancing around the circle. Drums kept a rolling beat, and the chanting of the dancers carried on the night air.

"You are to sit as a guest with Kicking Dog," she said as they walked toward the celebration.

Slocum used the crutch to keep the weight off his injured leg. The calf was still painfully sore, and he had accepted the fact that it would be that way for some time. At least it was not infected and appeared to be healing. As he moved toward the celebration, he had some reservations. From his experiences with the Sioux in the past, he knew the obvious shortage of buffalo left in this land would anger many of the tribes. Some of the men in particular would brood and then get vocal, especially if fortified with firewater. They would need someone to blame for their plight, and he would be the leading candidate. He rested on the crutch for a brief second. It would have been nice to have had some more rye whiskey. Then he wouldn't give a damn about his sore leg or what the Sioux said.

"Kicking Dog is a good man," she said.

"Nice enough," Slocum admitted.

"He brought my husband's body back for me to place on a platform."

"I am sure that was some comfort," he said, recalling her story of how a rifle accident during a hunt had taken her man. How she had rushed off to be alone after the funeral to mourn his death. To share his pain, she had cut off the first joint of her index finger with a knife. Then the pangs of his son's arrival had begun to cramp her. In fear, this being her first-born, and afraid of the possibility of losing it too, she'd rushed off in panic to find help with her delivery.

"I should move on soon," he said, looking ahead at the flames licking the sky over the gathering.

"You cannot stand on it. Stay until it is better."

"But other men may think you are tainted having kept a white man in your tepee. You will need to take a man. You're young and with a child to feed."

She wrinkled her nose at him. "I need time. Besides, it is none of their business who sleeps on my robes."

"I only worry for your future."

"When Man Dances was killed, my life was over. Now I am reborn and will live another life. Like the child, I came into a new world at the same time and you delivered me also."

"Putting a helluva lot of responsibility on me," he said, and shook his head in disapproval. Out of breath again and resting for a moment on the crutch, he discovered he was a lot weaker than he had supposed.

"The Great Spirit Woman sent you for a reason."

"Yes, so I could get to Montana."

She shifted the papoose board with a small hunch of her back, and pushed her firm breasts against the beaded front of the buckskin blouse. "You will see, you will see that she has a plan."

Whatever the Great Spirit had in mind, he wished he knew. His scalp itched all the time, and the hair on the back of his neck straightened from time to time in these people's presence. It was like walking through a cage of lions. With his injured leg, it didn't make him feel any more secure.

At last, he managed to reach his place of honor, to sit on the robes and blankets beside Kicking Dog. The chief acknowledged him as he leaned forward to gorge himself on a buffalo bone and let the juices run down in thin streams from the corners of his mouth.

A squaw came by and offered Slocum large portions of browned meat on a slab tray. He chose one, nodded his thanks to her, and began to eat. The sweet hot meat tasted good. It drew the saliva into his mouth, and he knew why the Indians held this animal's flesh in such high regard—it was their substance of life, besides being so delicious to eat. Diet made the individual. A horse on good grass grew tall, and little grass made a stunted animal. These Sioux were tall people overall, with plenty of dark-eyed children scurrying about at the edge of the fire's light. The buffalo was their god and provider; his disappearance was bound to upset them.

"You like her?" Kicking Dog elbowed him when Betty went past, stomp-dancing in a group of other women.

"She is a good person."

Kicking Dog nodded, and went back to devouring more meat.

"Her husband was a brave man," the chief offered between mouthfuls. "I was sad when he was shot."

"Accident, huh?"

Kicking Dog nodded absently, his dark eyes watching the dancers passing by. "The gun was cocked." He shrugged his great shoulders as if there was nothing he could do about it. "So when Yellow Deer slammed it down on the butt, it went off and shot her man in the face."

Slocum agreed to be cordial. "What is her name in Sioux?"

"White Swan."

"That suits her better than Betty."

Kicking Dog grinned at him pleased, then nodded and said her name in the guttural syllables of his own language.

"White Swan is fine," Slocum said, and took another chunk of buffalo from the woman's tray.

"Would you join us in the hunt tomorrow?"

"Would I make any of your men angry?"

"Who can say?"

"If you have invited me, I will be pleased to help you hunt."

Kicking Dog waved a half-eaten bone at him. "I will handle the angry ones."

"I am not here to make them mad."

The chief paused before taking another bite, looking mildly at Slocum. "I knew that when I met you. You are a strange white man. You are not afraid, but you aren't like a grizzly bear either. Most white men have to show they are tough. You wear that shirt well."

"I am your guest," Slocum said, and took a bite of meat.

"You will be treated as one."

"Thank you." He busied himself with eating. Indians considered it rude to stare at another person, and to do so could bring out the worst in unruly ones looking for an opportunity to cause trouble.

At last full to the brim, Slocum refused any more from the tray the woman repeatedly refilled, brought by, and presented. She moved on. The stomp-dancers grew louder. Obviously, some had found stronger liquid refreshment besides the tea served to Slocum.

A buck with his face streaked in yellow and red paint moved from the dancers to stand over Slocum. Anger drew his facial features into tight lines. Eyes squinted, mouth compressed, he looked ready to breathe fire.

"Who are you?" he demanded of Slocum.

Kicking Dog frowned and waved the man away. Then, with sharp words in Sioux, he berated the man. For a long second, the man acted as if the chief were not even there, all his animosity centered on Slocum. His hand was on the handle of the knife sheathed at his waist.

Then, with a great effort, but still showing physical prowess, Kicking Dog sprang to his feet and began shouting a tirade of words in the man's face. No doubt the chief's anger was enough to deter the man, for he looked haughtily at both Slocum and Kicking Dog, then left.

The chief sat down and scowled. "He don't want you to go hunt with us."

"Thinks I will taint the hunt?"

"No, he wants White Swan for himself." Kicking Dog shook his head to dismiss the matter. "She won't have him.

He treats his other wives badly and chases young girls who he gives gifts to."

"What is his name?"

"Red Hawk."

"I will remember him. Would I displease these people if I returned to the tepee? My leg is uncomfortable."

"How did you hurt it?" Kicking Dog frowned as if he had forgotten the story.

"Three drunk Lakota boys attacked me." Slocum motioned toward the south. "One got an arrow in me."

"They found plenty of courage in a whiskey bottle," Kicking Dog said knowingly. "It is worse than anything else that your people have brought here. Worse than the guns that shoot our buffalo at great distance, worse than the disease they put in the cunts of our loose women, even worse than the coughing disease or the belly sickness called cholera. Whiskey will kill more of my people than all of that." He dropped his chin as if in defeat. "They become walking dead when they take it."

Slocum waited for the man to look at him and give him permission to be excused.

"Go rest your leg and if you feel strong enough, ride with us and we will bring down food for my people."

Slocum agreed, and pushed himself to his feet. Then, using the crutch, he spun around to leave the back way. The dancers had worked themselves into a frenzy. Despite the cool night wind, they were sweaty-faced as they exhorted each other. He hobbled off into the long shadows of the tepees, avoiding snarling dogs that bristled at his approach, and moved toward White Swan's lodge.

Halfway around the camp he heard the rustle of leather soles on the grass. He paused, wishing for his Colt, and considered the smaller one in his boot. Whoever it was was half running, and would soon round the large tepee.

"Slocum?"

His heart stopped, and then he realized it was White Swan. Relieved, he closed his eyes for moment and took a deep breath. She hurried to him.

"Is your leg hurting?"

"Some."

"I will make some willow tea at the tepee for you."

"Why don't you stay and dance with your friends. You were having fun."

"I forgot for a little while I am a widow and that it might not be proper to enjoy myself too much."

"He would have enjoyed himself if he was here."

Her braids danced when she bobbed her head. She hitched up the papoose on her back, and gently turned Slocum by the arm toward the tepee. He leaned on the crutch and made his way with her.

The sounds of the drums and voices of the celebration carried on the night wind as he leaned on the crutch and swung his sore leg forward. She and the papoose waited every few steps for his slow progress. At last they reached the lodge. He leaned the crutch against it, dropped to his good knee, and scooted inside the opening on the buffalo-robe floor.

He removed his hat and combed his fingers through his hair. The sharp scent of the dying fire rose in his nostrils as she stirred it to heat water for tea. Then, in the shadowy light, she removed her blouse over her head, exposing her long shiny breasts filled with milk to let the infant suckle.

"Kicking Dog says your real name is White Swan."

She agreed.

"I will call you that," he said.

She busied herself helping the babe find nourishment.

"He wants me to go hunting with them tomorrow," Slocum said.

He could see her stop and blink at his words.

"But your leg—"

"I'll ride the dun and be careful."

"But it hurts you."

"Hurts me here, hurts me out there. Maybe I can help them kill some buffalo. Kicking Dog acts worried about a food supply for winter."

"What if some buck tries to kill you?"

"Like Red Hawk?"

"Yes, Red Hawk, he is coward enough."

"He wants to marry you."

"Hmm," she said in disapproval.

He wanted to laugh at her show of anger. Obviously the admiration was not mutual. She fixed Slocum's tea and handed him the small tin cup.

"This isn't some kind of potion to put me under a spell, is it?"

She laughed. "Maybe I should and stop you from going hunting."

He sipped the tea and looked into her liquid eyes in the firelight as she knelt before him. Her presence, closeness, and exposed long breasts made his guts roil. His leg stopped hurting, as if it wasn't there any longer, and he considered making love to her. His heart quickened. He wanted to reach out, smother her lips with his, taste the honey of her mouth, then find the bottom of her womb.

A sharp pain struck him like lightning when he shifted onto his bad leg, and he winced. Cold chills ran down his neck and spread over the skin of his shoulder underneath the shirt. The leg was still as sore as a boil, and throbbed again. He sipped more of her tea, and she went to her side of the fire pit.

4

Slocum stood outside the tepee venting his bladder in the early morning coolness. Already birds were making calls, and the ducks were busy at the lake. A thin slip of purple marked the eastern horizon. He could hear the young boys bringing in the horse herd they had tended all night. It would be a good day for the hunt. The sky was clear overhead. Perhaps the wind would not be so strong. Finished pissing, he buttoned his pants. She had sewn back the rip he'd cut open to tend to his wound. His tender leg held some weight for the first time, and that made him feel better. He wanted to be able to stand the ride and prove his worth to some of the skeptical bucks around the camp.

White Swan fed him some thick buffalo broth with wild turnips for breakfast. Then she rushed off to bring him his dun. That was traditionally a woman's job in a Lakota camp. She would return with his warhorse.

He had cleaned and oiled the Winchester. While not a long-range cannon like the Sharps .50-caliber, it would bring down a buffalo. He flirted with the baby in the papoose, tickled its chin, and made faces at it. The small face screwed up as if it wanted to say something.

She ducked inside and picked up his saddle and pads before he could protest. By the time he managed to get outside, she

22

was fixing the latigos. He put the rifle in the scabbard and limped around beside her.

As his shoulder touched hers, she looked at him. With a flash of anger in her dark eyes, she jerked the cinch tight and compressed her lips.

"You are as big a fool as any Lakota I know. Your pride won't let you heal that leg."

"I'll be fine."

"You can't outrun a wounded *wetonka*. You remember that. I won't cry for you if you are killed. I won't cut off my fingers for you." Then she faced him. "Like hell I won't."

He caught her arm and despite her struggling, drew her up on her toes. "This is what white men do to their women when they leave to go on a hunt."

His lips closed on her mouth and her eyes widened in shock. Then, finished kissing her, he straightened and grinned.

Her fingertips flew to her lips and she seemed in shock as she touched them.

"They call it a kiss," he said. "Think on it. You can have more if you want." He reached up, took the saddle horn in both hands, and bounded into the stirrup, swung his tender leg over, and put his boot in the other stirrup. Good, he could go hunt. She pushed her shoulder against his leg as she caught the bridle rein. When she'd stopped the dun, she looked up at him.

"I want more—later."

He nodded, and when she stepped back, he set the dun in short lope. No time to be late on his first hunt with the Lakota. He looked back at the tall girl. His kiss had touched her more deeply than he had imagined it would.

The hunters, some two dozen by his count, ranged from old men with gray hair to boys. Some of the hunters carried repeating rifles; most had trade weapons. Some had Hawkens, the better powder-and-ball models. Others carried old muskets, and some even used single-shot cartridge models. A few bucks had only bows and arrows. Slocum knew that kind of hunting was fading fast with the introduction of firearms to the Plains Indians. The close horse-and-rider contact required to make a killing shot with bow and arrow had fallen from favor among the tribes. Yet it was still considered an extreme act of bravery.

Slocum saw Red Hawk ahead in the party, and kept to himself at the rear. If Kicking Dog wanted him, he'd ride up there. Otherwise, taking a less obvious place seemed the thing to do.

After an hour's ride, scattered black dots began to appear on the prairie. Not many, perhaps a dozen. Certainly not like the old days, when huge herds several miles wide took several days to pass a point.

Kicking Dog rode back through the riders to talk to Slocum.

"Slo-cum, would you and some of my best marksmen ride south and lay in wait? When we attack them, we will come into the wind. When they stampede, they won't smell you until they are right on you. Then it will be too late. Shoot as many as you can that get away from us. The women will be here soon to skin and butcher them."

Slocum agreed, and Kicking Dog shouted for two men, a middle-aged man with a Winchester called Snow Bear and another, younger one, Brown Badger, who had a sports rifle, to go along with him. The three rode south. They went wide so their scent would be out of the buffalos' noses. The two Indians spoke in Sioux as they rode along.

Snow Bear indicated a place for Slocum to get down where he would have a shot if the buffalo followed the course of the land and swept past them through this basin. The older man sent Brown Badger down the way, and then took their horses over the hill.

Slocum had his rifle, a pocket full of cartridges, and some jerky to chew on, and bellied down in the short grass to wait. It was not long until he heard shots in the distance. He shared a nod with Brown Badger and readied his rifle. More shots came, and then the drum of hooves in the distance. The yipping cries of the hunters carried above the increasing wind.

The first buffalo crested the rise and headed down the swale as planned. Slocum held his fire, knowing a head shot would never stop it. The skull was too thick to penetrate, and the animal's brain too small for a bullet to find. The rolling lope of the shaggy beast bore it closer. Slocum sighted in on the animal's chest, fired, and within three strides it collapsed on its side and slid in the grass.

Three more were coming. Seeing the downed one, the bisons detoured to the right, and Brown Badger wounded one, breaking its shoulder and causing it to limp to a stop. Slocum decided the others were by this time too far away to waste ammunition on. Then a yearling calf came barreling over the ridge. His tongue hanging out and his nostrils flared open, he raced after the others.

Out of the wash, Snow Bear charged on horseback for the animal. In hot pursuit he drew up beside it. Slocum watched in amazement. The old man was riding in close to make his kill, like a bow hunter. Snow Bear leaned over and shot the calf in the chest. His horse veered at that moment, or lost his footing, and collided with the buffalo.

The two animals went end over end, and Snow Bear was thrown hard to the ground. Slocum rose to rush to his aid. His sore leg pained him, but he was more concerned about the older warrior's safety. Slocum was fifty feet from where Snow Bear lay, not moving, when the wounded bull spotted him. Dragging his front leg, the enraged animal charged.

Slocum looked around. There was no place to go, and worse, his leg was giving out. The bull was making better time covering the distance between them despite the animal's disability. There was no way to try and outrun him. Nothing to do but take aim and hope a chest shot would stop him.

A puff of dust flew out of the bull's brown fur from Slocum's first bullet. With the second round levered in, Slocum could hear the animal's strained breathing. Another shot, and the pounding of the buffalo's hooves was shaking the ground under Slocum's boot soles. Two more quick shots, and the bull skidded his bloody nose in the ground fifteen feet from Slocum's smoking gun, then fell over on his side.

Brown Badger came running, and Slocum knew that the last shot had stopped the big brute. The man babbled in Sioux and shook his head as if impressed. He cautiously poked the downed animal with the muzzle of his gun, and, satisfied it was dead, nodded to Slocum.

They both hurried to where the dazed Snow Bear sat on his butt.

"Tough sumbitch!" Snow Bear pointed at Slocum. Brown Badger agreed and nodded his approval.

Slocum shook his head. "You and Brown Badger are the hunters. I am the helper."

Snow Bear translated in Sioux for Brown Badger, and the younger man shook his head, then began to speak in a profusion of words.

"He says you are the brave man to not have run from the *wetonka*," Snow Bear translated.

Slocum shook his head to dismiss the praise, and helped Snow Bear up. The old man acted as if he was no worse off than bruised, though he did limp some when they went to look at the large bull that had caused all the trouble.

Soon a party of men and several squaws with horses and travois came to join them. Brown Badger had fetched Slocum's dun for him. Slocum stood beside the horse and prepared to mount up. He was ready to ride back when Red Hawk drove his buffalo pony toward him.

"You bad omen! Cause me not to kill *wetonka*. I will kill you, white eyes." He raised up his rifle, decorated with copper tacks but at that instant, his horse ducked sideways enough to force him to jerk on the jaw bridle. The move was enough. Slocum stepped in, grabbed his moccasin, and shoved him off the horse. When the piebald shied away, Red Hawk fell to the ground and blinked, his mouth open. Slocum held the Colt in his fist pointed at the buck.

The single-shot rife was only inches from the buck's fingers. The wind ruffled the fringe on his shirt. Somewhere a raven called, and a weary horse snorted through his nose.

"Enough!" Kicking Dog said, and rode his horse up.

"It's up to him," Slocum said. "He started it."

The words the chief gave Red Hawk in Lakota sounded like a father telling a son the rules of life. Kicking Dog's rules, to be specific. When he finished, Red Hawk took his rifle and horse, looked sullenly at Slocum, and rode away.

Kicking Dog turned his bay around, then paused and came back.

"You are a guest of my people. He should have better manners. Next time kill him."

5

It was time to celebrate. Bloody-fisted women ate raw liver as they disemboweled the downed buffalo. They fed it to the men, who stood around and bragged about their skills. Raw heart and liver became the treat of the day. Slocum ate some to be cordial.

"There will be food this winter," White Swan said with a glint in her brown eyes, and wiped the rivulet of sweat from her face on the back of her hand. Then she grasped the woolly hide in one hand, and began to slash the furry cover away from the yellow fat layer and meat. He watched her work bent over, with two other women's keen knives also peeling away the hide, until the mountainous carcass needed to be turned. Several more women rushed over to help them. They flopped the bull over on the other side, and the skinners resumed their work.

A huge fire was built at sundown, and the cooking begun. Slocum was amazed at the amount of wood the Sioux found for this purpose. Except for some small pines and cedars on the ridges, the only other trees of any size grew along the rivers. Their wood source was unknown to him, but somehow they always managed to have a good supply for their dances and feasts.

She came to him with her papoose. The copper smell of slaughter clung to her. "There is much work yet to do."

28

"I will hold the child."

"No, it is too dark, we can't see. I want to go back and bathe." She tossed her head in the direction of the camp.

"We can ride my horse double."

"No, I can walk. You ride."

"We will miss the celebration."

"We won't need one," she said softly, and looked away as if embarrassed.

"I will go back only if you will ride behind me on the dun."

She shook her head in disapproval. "I will ride with you, but I am very filthy."

"It won't hurt the horse."

Her giggling was loud, and she put her fingers to her mouth to suppress it. Still, the snickers escaped, and soon she was laughing aloud. Then, as if she feared someone had noticed her, she drew the blanket up to hide her face behind it.

"Aren't widows supposed to laugh?" Slocum swung up and offered her his hand to help her up.

"Of course not." She seated herself behind him and then threw her arms around him. Her firm breasts bored two holes in his back.

"Ready?" he asked.

"Yes."

He booted the dun for camp, and looked to the first stars of evening for help. His heart raced, and the prospects of the night ahead made his stomach churn. They reached the camp, dogs heralded their welcome, and a few elder Sioux came out to nod at them. One old woman asked White Swan about the kill, and when she heard how many animals had been slaughtered, she gave a loud yelp.

They reached the lake, and the rising half-moon reflected off the water. She slid from the dun and set the papoose aside. He undid the cinch and let the pony breath. Quickly she untied the bedroll on the back and unfurled it on the grass. He took the saddle off, set it on the horn, and turned the dun loose to move off and graze, satisfied the pony would not roam far.

She stripped off her blouse, then shed her skirt and leg-

gings. Undressed, she ran down the slope, made a leap, and
dove into the lake. He watched her swim in the moonlight,
the glow on her slick wet skin as her arms cut through the
water in graceful movement.

He toed off his boots, shucked his socks, vest, and shirt,
then his pants and underwear. His sore leg impeded his charge
into the water's edge, but he soon was in up to his waist. The
lukewarm liquid felt good, and he struck out to swim a few
yards. When he returned and waded toward her, she stood up
before him with water streaming from her proud breasts, cap-
ped with the dark nipples that fed her son.

Their mouths met and they clutched each other. It was the
hungry grasp of two starving people, her body molded to him.
He tasted the sweetness of her mouth. It spun his brain like
a dust devil, with the lushness of her body pressed to his.
The growing hardness of his erection reached skin-taut readiness. His hands raced over her, feeling the muscles and the
shapely form of her body.

Then she led him from the lake, the cool night air sweeping
over his wet skin. It wasn't a time for words. Both knew what
they wanted, and he barely felt the soreness in his leg as he
lay down with her on the bedroll.

He rose to get on top of her, winced at his injured limb,
then separated her shapely legs. The same copper legs he'd
seen spread open the day he found her. The ones he had never
forgotten. She pulled him down on top of her, their mouths
locked with each other. His throbbing erection, directed into
her gates, entered her, and she gasped at his intrusion.

His aching hips sought her, she hunched her back for him,
and they meshed as one. The world spun. His urgency sped
him faster and faster, until they were both gasping for breath
and neither one wanted it to stop. Soon, despite the night's
coolness, they became slick with sweat as their bellies rubbed
together with enough friction to start a fire.

At last, the cords in her neck drew tight and a cry escaped
her open mouth. He felt the hot rush of fluid spill out of her,
and at last the long-held flood surged up his dick and flew
out like a spewing geyser. They fell in a heap on top of his
bedroll.

When he awoke, she was sitting up and feeding the papoose. It was a still night. He looked at the Big Dipper, and decided it must be near midnight.

"Are you sorry we left the celebration?" she asked.

He stretched luxuriously on his back and considered her. The cool wind swept his bare skin and made him shiver. "No."

She giggled.

There would be much pemmican when all the meat was dry. The chokecherries were making plenty of fruit along the watercourses. The ripe sweet cherries would be smashed, seeds and all, then mixed with powder-dry buffalo meat and stuffed into intestines, and sealed with melted tallow. It would keep for years. Excitement filled the camp as the meat processing began again the next day.

White Swan and the other women worked day and night. Slocum's leg made more progress toward healing while he loafed in camp, though he knew the hunt had set his recovery back some. There was little time for anything but work for the women. He watched the papoose while she labored; she returned at times throughout the day and suckled it. Late at night she came to the tepee, fell asleep in her robes, slept a few hours, and was soon back at the consuming task. The older women in camp cooked and served the men food.

To keep occupied, Slocum cleaned his firearms. He oiled and worked over his saddle, until he was bored with sitting around. The ever-present smoke from the drying process whipped through the camp. Aside from an occasional dogfight over some poor bitch in heat, which meant some buck had to get up and force the dogs apart by thrashing them, not much else happened.

At the end of a week, Kicking Dog came to see Slocum, who was sitting on the ground. Slocum wondered what the chief had on his mind. He was a large man, but his braids were short, the ends barely brushing his broad shoulders.

"The Blackfeet used to be a powerful people," he said. "They controlled all of this land. Then they took smallpox and great numbers of them died. They say that the Blackfeet have the best horses, better than the Pawnee once had."

Slocum nodded. He understood the implications of the man's words. Kicking Dog's larder was now full enough that the tribe would not starve. The Sioux's fancy had turned to horse stealing.

"How far away is their camp?" Slocum asked.

"Maybe a week's ride or less."

"How many would go?"

"A few. I must leave some to guard the women and children."

Slocum agreed. "What would you ask of me?"

"To ride with us."

For a long moment, he considered the request, wet his lips, and wondered if he belonged with a band of horse thieves, especially Sioux horse thieves. His leg was healed enough—still sore when he walked too much, but he could do his part. It would be a challenge to go and do something he had never done before. Besides, he knew it was out of respect that the chief had asked him to go along.

"When will you leave?" Slocum asked.

"In a few days."

"I will decide by then."

Kicking Dog nodded as if that was enough of an answer. White Swan had told Slocum that all the talk at the celebration was about his bravery and the wounded bull's charge. He scoffed at her words, and told her the only reason he'd stood his ground that day was because he couldn't run on his bad leg.

She'd laughed at his words and then wrinkled her nose. "Sioux know bravery."

"What about Snow Bear, who took on the buffalo from horseback?"

"Showing off. It was only a calf."

"When I am that old, I will be in a rocking chair."

"I don't see you in a rocking chair." She'd shaken her head and stared at him, as if she did not believe that that would ever happen to him.

"I'll probably not live that long," he'd replied.

She returned in mid-afternoon from working on the buffalo

skins, set the papoose beside him, and began a fire of buffalo chips outside the tepee.

"They speak of stealing Blackfeet horses," she said, as if too busy to look at him.

"Men talk of such things?" He lifted the papoose and smiled at the baby, who made sucking faces at him. The poor thing must be hungry.

"They want the brave white man to join them."

"Be different. I never stole any Blackfeet horses."

"So you have told them you would go with them!"

"No. I was going to talk with you first."

"Me? I am not your wife, your mother-in-law."

"Oh."

She scowled at him, then stood up and crossed the space between them. Hands on her hips, she stood with her feet apart. "It would be a foolish thing for you to do."

"Sioux do it all the time. Go on horse raids."

"Yes, but—"

"But I am white man."

She snatched up the whimpering papoose, raised her blouse, and force a nipple in the infant's mouth. Her anger seethed, and he wanted to laugh, but suppressed his urge. It was far too serious a matter to her for him to snicker at.

"Do you wish to die?" she asked.

"You think because you lost your man that I will be next?"

Her eyes softened and turned liquid with tears. "Since the day I found you I have feared losing you."

"A few old Blackfeet won't get me."

"How can you be certain? You must use the sweat lodge and clear yourself. If you must act like a Sioux, then you must take the precautions of one."

"I know little of the ways. Maybe your medicine won't work on me."

"I will show you then," she said, and switched the baby to her other breast. "It will work."

He agreed with a nod of his head. His mind was more on making love to her again when the sun set than on spending his time in a sweat lodge. Whatever, he would be ready to ride with Kicking Dog, and he would regret the whole time that he had left her luscious body at the tepee.

6

The foggy hot interior of the lodge drew a phlegm-loaded cough from Slocum's throat. His nose burned from the strong sage aroma that permeated the air. His naked body slick with his own sweat, he sat on the slimy hide and listened to Snow Bear's incantments: words that sounded like a prayer, but more forceful. The light was so poor in the lodge, he could only make out the outline of the man's head as he waved a willow branch in the four directions and rambled on with his Sioux song.

Slocum hoped the ritual would end soon, but it went on for hours. White Swan and other women brought more hot rocks to sizzle the water in the great iron kettle. This special vessel was used only for such ceremonies, never cooked in nor used to bathe or drink water from. To Slocum, it looked like a lard-rendering kettle, but he'd kept still when she explained the sacredness of the container. The fresh load of steam in the lodge caused him to cough some more.

The torture lasted for hours. Then at sundown, Snow Bear led him outside. The wind on Slocum's bare skin cooled him and he felt depleted. Red rays streaked the far horizon. They went to the moon lake and washed away the sweat and grime of the day-long session. Slocum hoped he had passed the test and was through.

"You must not eat anything from a can," Snow Bear said, "until we return."

Simple enough. Slocum agreed and rinsed off his arms, then rose to wade out, satisfied that that was no problem. He hadn't seen anything canned since he'd left North Platte, Nebraska, over two weeks before.

On shore, he pulled on his pants, gathered his clothing, and went to White Swan's tepee. She had roasted an antelope that he had shot the day before. There were others gathered there for the meal. Some older people, who nodded, and three young couples. One was her younger sister and her man. The two women resembled each other. The sister's husband Slocum had seen on the hunt.

Everyone was quiet, waiting for him to take a place at the head of the blanket.

"How was it?" she asked, serving him a large hunk of meat on a slab of bark.

"Hot and steamy."

"Did you learn much?"

"Yes, that I like it better out here."

Some translated it to others around the circle. First the women giggled, then they all laughed. One of the toothless women reached out, slapped his arm, and said something in Sioux to him. Slocum looked at White Swan for an answer.

She looked at the sky for help, then translated it as if she shouldn't be speaking. "Her husband said the same damn thing when he first went to one, and he never liked them."

Several laughed, and then they explained it to the rest, which brought more hoots. Slocum felt a little smug. There were even Sioux who found the ordeal in the sweat lodge just that—something to endure. Good, he wasn't alone in this camp. Everyone feasted on the antelope and liked it. He could see the grins on their faces and greasy mouths.

Later, he and White Swan snuggled together naked in her night robes. He could see a few stars out through the open smoke hole above them. Unable to control his hands, he kneaded her flesh and savored the muscular foundation under her sleek skin. It was only minutes until she captured his erection and guided him on top of her.

"What will you do sleeping alone without me?" she asked.

"Dream of you."

"Ha, your hand will be raw from jacking off when you return."

"No, I'll save it all for you."

"Then I will be too sore to walk."

"Does it hurt you?" he asked, concerned about their frequency.

"I wouldn't tell you if it did," she said, and spread her legs wide for him.

The night before they left, Kicking Dog had told them they must travel light. Dried jerky, a blanket to sleep in, ammunition, and weapons would be all they needed, plus some lariats to lead their captive horses back with. In the predawn, Slocum took the reins from White Swan and kissed her goodbye.

She shook her head in disapproval at his leaving and backed away. He swung up on the dun. No time to back out now. He was off to steal the Blackfeet horses. He waved, and booted the dun toward the center of camp to meet the others. Time to be gone.

Five of them made up the party: Kicking Dog, Snow Bear, a boy called Same Foot, and Brown Badger, in addition to Slocum. They pushed their ponies hard, and Slocum's leg ached by mid-afternoon when they stopped at a small steam to water and rest their mounts. Kicking Dog avoided settlements and even ranches. He wanted their presence as little known as possible so as not to warn the Blackfeet.

Slocum wondered how far away the Blackfeet were. Miles were nothing to Indians. A day's travel meant anywhere from forty to sixty miles on horseback the way they traveled, light and in a hurry. Unfamiliar with the sweeping northern plains, Slocum had few points to guide him. The second day they crossed the railroad, and he knew they must be in Dakota Territory.

"We will find them soon," Kicking Dog said, satisfied they were drawing near the region of the Blackfeet.

But what they found at first proved soberly disappointing.

There were old camps with tattered tepee covers, the remnants of the skins flapping in the wind. Long abandoned and empty places where many had died. Kicking Dog did not ride into these camps, as if they might be contaminated, but circled them. No one spoke, as if they were sacred places. They rode on.

Had this haunting experience happened once, Slocum would have dismissed it. The deserted ghost camps became more plentiful the closer they pushed to the Missouri.

"Maybe all the Blackfeet have died?" Brown Badger asked, riding close to Slocum's stirrup.

"It don't look like there's lots of them left," Slocum agreed. They rode on in silence. Kicking Dog had said little, the wrinkles in his forehead growing deeper.

When they camped that evening, seated at their small fire in a circle, the chief finally spoke. "Perhaps there are no Blackfeet." He used his hand to cut the air. "None left in all the land. And this trip is a waste. But where have their horses gone? Did they die too?"

"Perhaps," Slocum said, "I could go to one of the outposts and ask. They wouldn't suspect me."

Kicking Dog agreed. "Be a good idea. I don't like to be gone so long from my people. If they are all dead, then we should go home."

Early the next morning, Slocum set out. He found a trading post by mid-morning, and dismounted before the crude log structure with low walls. He hitched his horse and chased the barking cur dogs away. A short Indian woman came to open the door and let him in. He ducked his head and stepped down into the room.

Two whiskered men in buckskin were seated at the table, and they looked at him critically and waved him over. They offered him some firewater from a crock, and he agreed to try it. The older of the two, with gray streaks in his beard, poured him some in a tin cup.

"Have a seat. What brings you up here?" the older one asked, setting the crock back on the table. "I'm Wyman, that's Carnaster."

Slocum nodded to the second man. "Looking to buy some Blackfeet horses."

"Hell, ain't you heard? They all died two years ago. Ain't more'n a piss pot of them left over in Montana."

"What happened to their horses?"

"Run off, gawdamned if I know. Do you?" Wyman asked Carnaster.

"I ain't seen any lately. They must have gone wild or the wolves ate them. Them sumsabitches bad now they ain't got enough buffalo to eat."

Slocum looked around. "Guess trading's slow."

"Slower than damn hell. Buffalo about all gone around here. We're fixing to go to Montana ourselves pretty soon."

"You don't know of any horses then around here?"

The two looked at each other, then shook their heads. Slocum downed their whiskey, thanked them, and rose. "Much obliged. I came a long ways for nothing, I guess."

"If you are looking for Blackfeet or their hosses, you damn sure did."

"Thanks," he said, and went outside. He was grateful to be out in the open air. Those two smelled worse than hogs. He would bet neither of them had had a bath since the year before, if then. Mounted on the dun, he headed south to join the Sioux.

"The Blackfeet are dead?" Kicking Dog asked in disbelief.

"Most of them," Slocum reported to the chief. "They said the few left were in Montana."

"We have seen no buffalo for days, no Blackfeet. It is a bad omen. We must return at once." Kicking Dog looked deeply concerned at the news.

Snow Bear nodded to Slocum. "I told him something is wrong. I feel it in my bones."

"Bones sometimes tell a lot," Slocum agreed. He studied the bloodred sky in the west and wondered what his bones told him. He considered White Swan and what she was doing. It would be good to be in her tepee and share her robes again.

They left by first light. Kicking Dog rode right by ranches, not bothering to disguise his travel. He wanted to return to his people as quickly as possible. A feeling of gloom began to prevail in the small party. The harder they rode, the more serious they became.

What once was to be a lighthearted horse-stealing expedition had turned to a concerned rush to get home and make sure that all was well there. The vulnerability of the camp and the people there became the pressing concern.

On the third day they drew near. Snow Bear mentioned that there was no smoke in the sky. Slocum agreed. Kicking Dog forced his spent horse to lope, and disappeared over the rise ahead of them.

When Slocum topped the ridge, he first noticed the yellow company flag fluttering in the wind, then the U.S. flag, the soliders' tents, and the wagons parked close by the village. Something had happened. Why was the military there? He shared a pensive look with the old man. Then the four of them rode side by side toward the camp.

7

"I have been searching for buffalo!" Kicking Dog shouted at the bearded civilian when Slocum reined up the dun close by them. "To feed my people. They can't live on the small lots of wormy pork and meal that your agency gives us in the spring and fall."

Slocum grasped the saddle horn and surveyed the situation. There was a shavetail officer, a lieutenant fresh out of West Point, no doubt, and a hard-looking sergeant who had seen plenty of action. Six soldiers with rifles were backing this tall man in the white shirt with the derby hat cocked on his head. Obviously, this was the Indian agent. He pulled on his pointed beard and frowned at Slocum.

"What's he doing here, selling guns or whiskey?" he demanded of Kicking Dog while pointing at Slocum.

"Neither. What are you doing here harassing this man?" Slocum demanded. He could see that the Sioux men they had left in camp were all sitting on the ground, obviously under some sort of arrest.

"My name is Harrington McFaye and I am the government's representative for this agency. And what are you doing here on Indian lands?"

"He's married to a Sioux woman," Kicking Dog said sharply.

"Oh," McFaye said. "Still, what's the nature of your business here?"

"Kicking Dog told you, looking for buffalo."

"I have reports to the contrary, that this band has been making raids on white wagon trains and ranches north of here."

"Mister, they've lied to you. We've been clear to the Missouri River looking for buffalo and we haven't harmed a pissant."

"What's your name?"

"Slocum, John Slocum."

"Well, Slocum, I am moving this whole village closer to the agency, so they can be counted and watched."

"Hold on a minute. These people have been minding their own business, making a living. There is nothing to hunt down there. Do you have food for them down there?"

"This is not a negotiable situation." McFaye's face reddened at Slocum's challenge.

"You're wrong, mister. Don't move them. They have hurt no one."

"I have reports of ranches burned, trains raided—"

"Lies!" Kicking Dog shouted, so loud the soldiers clutched their rifles. "All lies, we have been hunting and curing much meat. The women have sought berries. We have made no attacks on anyone."

"You can lie until the sun sets, Kicking Dog," McFaye said. "You and your band are moving closer to the agency in the morning. Those are my orders. Lieutenant Crane, tell them how and when you want them ready to move."

"Yes, sir." The small officer clicked his heels together.

"This is Sioux land," Kicking Dog said to the uniformed man. "I signed a treaty to live on this land, to hunt on it, and to feed my family. . . ."

Slocum shook his head in disgust and walked away. There was no talking to a post. That officer was like one. He had his orders from McFaye, and there was not one damn thing would change his mind. Where was White Swan? He headed through the camp, and saw the concern written on the brown faces of the women, who were using their hands to block the glare of the setting sun as they watched the proceedings.

"How long have they been here?" he asked White Swan when she came out of the tepee. He hugged her. She shook with revulsion in his arms, and he looked down into her eyes. Then, as if it had all been too much, she buried her face in his vest and shook her head.

"Two days," she said at last. "What can we do? They say we must go down to the agency and stay there and be counted."

"Not much else to do unless you want to fight them."

"I would fight them," she said, the edge of defiance in her tone.

"Many women and children would be killed, and then they would send more soldiers and punish all of you."

She dropped her chin. "I hoped you would come back and help us. You brought no horses?" She looked back at the military encampment.

"There are no Blackfeet."

"What?" Her eyes flew open.

"They have all died or have gone to Montana. We saw many ghost camps. It was not a good trip." He didn't tell her that in all their travels they saw no buffalo either. The news of the Blackfeet's demise was enough of a shock.

"Come, I have some food inside."

He looked back at the soldiers and the prisoners seated on the ground. The situation was very volatile. With a disapproving shake of his head, he ducked and went inside.

"It has been very tense here," she said, dishing out some stew in a turtle shell for him. "I feared some of the younger men would begin to shoot when they were told what to do."

"The soldiers told them?"

"Yes, with guns ready."

"This McFaye, has he been agent here long?"

"No, he is new. We had heard he would make everyone live beside the agency and be counted."

"Obviously, he has the backing of the military."

"What can we do?"

Slocum considered the rich stew in the bowl. It would taste

good after the many days of dry jerky. "Go and be counted."
He busied himself eating.

"Mr. Slocum?" It was officer's voice outside the tepee. Slocum exchanged a frown with her. He set the bowl down and
rose to go outside. What did the man want?

"Yes," Slocum said, emerging from the tent and seeing two
soldiers and the officer.

"If this band would promise to be at the agency in three to
four days, I am prepared to let them make their way there."

"Smart idea. What did Kicking Dog say to that?"

"I am asking you—"

"Hey, I am not the chief here. I am a guest of these people."

"He is in no mood to talk to anyone. I felt you might talk
sense to him. McFaye is insistent they move there. I have to
follow his orders. I have no reason to doubt you or the chief's
word about your absence. My orders are—"

"Wait. I understand military-civilian relations. But first you
go up and release those prisoners as a sign of good faith.
Then I will go try and talk to Kicking Dog."

"I can't do that."

Slocum looked at the last blood of the sunset, shook his
head, and started to go back in the tepee.

"Wait."

"No waiting, Lieutenant Crane. You want my help, then
you must show trust. Those men being held up there are an
insult to trust."

Crane chewed on his thin lower lip for a second. "All right,
but I expect this to work."

"So do I, Lieutenant. So do I."

The officer gave orders to his sergeant to release the prisoners, and then shook his head. "This may cost me."

"It may save some lives," Slocum said.

"We are at an impasse here. I hope you can convince Kicking Dog that he must move."

"I'll try." Slocum felt White Swan's hand on his arm as
she stood slightly behind him. It was a sign of approval and
commitment from her. Perhaps they could convince the village and Kicking Dog. He hoped so.

Slocum started back in the tepee, and the officer caught him. "Aren't you going now?"

"When the council is called, I will ask to speak."

"When will they do that?"

"As soon as they all are free to have one, I guess." Slocum's hard glare at the man's restraining hand forced him to let go.

"Slocum, this better work."

"No one wants it any more than I do, Lieutenant." That said, he went inside the tepee and took a place on the floor.

White Swan joined him and sat nearby, lifted the papoose board, raised her blouse, and fed the infant. There was no need for words. Both knew that the fate of the camp hung in the balance. Either obey or have war, and the next move was the chief's.

The small fire cast an orange light on White Swan's features. The worry was reflected in her brown eyes, and she licked her lips often while the baby noisily fed. When he was finished, she unwrapped him, cleaned away the cattail packing that absorbed his excrement, and washed him. She handed him, dried and squirming, to Slocum to hold.

He grinned and cooed to the child, bouncing him around and making him grin. The infant had grown much stronger in Slocum's absence. He would be a large man someday. She repacked the bundle with fresh cattail fluff, and took him back to put in his board.

Someone outside cleared their throat, and Slocum went to see. It was Snow Bear. The older man had taken a seat beside the entrance.

"Come in," Slocum offered.

"No, I hoped not to disturb you. I was once young, and recalled coming home after so many days. I would have killed anyone who disturbed me in the first while." In the twilight Slocum saw the man's sly grin.

"I have had no time for such," Slocum said. "There have been others come here to talk too." Slocum sat down cross-legged beside the man. The tender leg complained, but he stood the pain.

Snow Bear nodded his head. "Yes, I saw the officer come here, and then the men were set free."

"I asked him in good faith to do that. No one wants to make a decision with guns to their head."

"Will they kill us at the agency?"

"I don't think so, if you mean shoot you."

Snow Bird nodded. "Will you come to the council?"

"If I am welcome."

"Kicking Dog wants you to come and talk to them. Since they were released, they think you have much power with these soldiers."

"I had a bluff was all."

"A bluff? What is that?"

"It is like the man who acts rich and has no wealth."

"Bluff," the man repeated. "Good thing it worked."

"I will be there after the others have talked," Slocum said. "They will have much to say. Send word and I will come."

"Ah, you will rest your ears." Snow Bear laid his hand on Slocum's shoulder. "I am ready to die here, but it would be foolish to have our women and children suffer for our haste."

"It is not our way alone we must think about."

"Agreed, my friend. I will tell them you respect their right to talk in council, and I will send a messenger when it is time for you to come."

Slocum rose, and they clapped each other on the shoulder. Snow Bear hurried for the campfire, an obvious limp in his right leg. The long ride had been taxing on the older man, but Slocum could recall his eyes when they rode around the ghost camps. Just the awareness that a whole tribe of people was gone, dead, or vanished had made Snow Bear's shoulders slump in dismay.

Before Slocum went back inside, he looked the camp over, and could see the growing fire's glow. There would be many to talk this night. They had much to get off their chests. Indignation and contempt would be in their speeches. Inside the tepee on his knees, he paused. He could see in the dim light that she was naked and her arms were stretched out for him.

His eyes shut to the problems of the council, he savored her supple body against his.

With his nose in her clean hair, he could smell the flowers of the prairie, and he closed his eyes.

8

"I will die here where we are first!" Kicking Dog shouted in English. The translations of the chief's oath were made to those who did not understand a word of it. There were nods of solemn approval around the circle on the sullen copper faces reflecting the fire's orange-red light.

"To die is honorable," Slocum said. "But we have ridden many days hard." He paused, and Snow Bear repeated the words in Sioux. Grateful the older man had taken on the task, he knew the words would be accurate.

"What did we find?" Slocum paused again. "We found the camp of your enemies, the Blackfeet, empty, except for their ghosts. I saw their tepee skins in rags blowing in the wind like pieces of fur on a dead horse's ribs after the wolves have feasted on him." Slocum dropped his gaze to the fire and waited for the translation. "Not one camp, not two, but more than I have fingers." He held them up to show them.

"Then I went to a trading post and asked the traders, 'Where are the Blackfeet?'" Snow Bear translated in Sioux. "'They are all dead except a few who went to Montana,' I was told." Slocum waited. "Then I asked, 'Where are their great horses? The big herds of wonderful, powerful paints.'" He paused for Snow Bird to translate, then said softly, "Gone too.

"You can be like the Blackfeet. You can become Blackfeet

47

tomorrow. But so will your wives and children."

Slocum sat down with that said. The voices rose in anger, and he saw it in their eyes, defiance and stone madness. Guttural words of the Lakota language rang in the night. These were men too filled with hatred to even make sense with. He sipped on some tea served by one of Kicking Dog's wives. He listened and waited. Like a raging fire, the anger had to sometimes be consumed before it could be controlled.

Even Kicking Dog could not settle them down so that only one spoke at a time. The chief shook his head at their outrage when he made eye contact with Slocum. Finally, some order was restored.

Snow Bear rose and began to speak. Slocum could not understand the strange words, but he knew what the gray-headed man told them. How he was haunted by the Blackfeet ghost camps and how powerful he'd always considered their enemy. Then the sage threw a small handful of gunpowder in the fire, and it exploded in a great burst of flame. Everyone looked in awe, not because they had not seen such displays before, but because the old man had undoubtedly told them that would be them—a flash in the fire and gone.

Then Snow Bear pointed at Slocum. "Will they kill us at the agency?" He repeated his question in Sioux.

Slocum shook his head. A sigh went out from the ring of men and they began to talk quietly.

"Can we have five days?" Kicking Dog asked Slocum.

"He said three or four. I will ask for five so we can finish the jerky and make the rest of the pemmican."

"We will come slow, pick berries and kill game, if we find any."

"I will go ask him for permission if the council wishes me to."

Kicking Dog asked them aloud and they nodded. Some were resistant, but they were prodded by others and it was unanimous. Slocum excused himself.

The night wind was cool on his face as he crossed the dark ground. He could see a light was on in the main tent. Before he reached the sentry, the man called out.

"That civilian Slocum is here, sir."

"Show him in."

"Go ahead, sir. The lieutenant is waiting."

"Thanks, Private."

He stepped inside, and the shavetail rose to his feet. "Good evening. You have news?"

"Yes. The village has agreed to go to the agency, but they want ten days."

"Ten days?"

"Sit down, Lieutenant. There are many berries ripening in this moon. They want to harvest them along the way. It will be the only sweetness in their lives for the coming year."

"I don't know whether McFaye will agree to that long."

"I guess they will be there for an extended time. What is ten days?"

"He expected me to have them there overnight."

"You didn't bring enough wagons or fast enough horses."

The lieutenant laughed aloud. "I am ready for a drink. Would you have one, Slocum?"

"Maybe two."

Crane paused in reaching for the bottle. "Was it that tough to convince them?"

"Not easy."

"Well, I could hear all the shouting over there. Took you long enough. I have my men sleeping in shifts, just in case."

"Where's McFaye?"

"Asleep in his tent, I guess." Crane poured them both drinks and shoved the cup toward Slocum. "I agree with you it's a mistake to do this."

"All those Sioux down there are mad as hornets and with nothing to hunt. If I was the man, I'd have left them scattered across the country so they can still find buffalo. Takes their minds off things. These people in this camp never attacked anyone. Why doesn't he go find the guilty renegades instead of punishing all the Sioux?"

"My orders are to back the agent, so he can manage the reservation."

"I know." Slocum took a good slug of the whiskey and closed his eyes. "We may all pay for this."

"You think it will cause an uprising?"

"I think it will sure send some peaceful bucks likes these to join the outsiders like Sitting Bull, Gall, Crazy Horse, and the others out there who are ignoring the reservation. McFaye needs to count that bunch, not these."

"Ten days was the best you could do?" Crane looked pained by the notion.

"They should arrive there in ten days. Will McFaye have enough provisions for all of them when they get there?"

"There are supposed to be cattle coming and wagons of goods."

"Skinny longhorns driven up here to replace the fat buffalo in their diet is like asking your soldiers to eat their shoe leather."

"Not my department. We have to eat those skinny cattle too."

"Let them graze a summer up here on this rich grass, they'd be a damn sight better."

"Yeah, but they don't last that long." Crane raised his cup in a toast, and Slocum met it. "To lots of fat beef."

"Amen."

It was later when Slocum returned to the council. Many had left, but others gathered around to hear the details. Slocum looked over the tired faces.

"Ten days to get there," he said, and held up both hands. They grunted in approval and nodded at his success.

"That is good," Kicking Dog said in gratitude.

"You can pick berries on the way," Slocum said, and grinned at him and Snow Bear. He suppressed a great yawn as he waved good night; he was tired enough to sleep ten days. His leg was sore, and he wanted to be in White Swan's arms and held.

The camp began to load in the morning. The army was gone, and with it the agent. Wagons and troopers had moved out with the dawn. With things returned to normal, the dogs began to fight over two separate bitches in heat. So the outbursts were all over the camp. White Swan worked on the bull robe that the men had awarded to Slocum. He sat in the morning sun and oiled his guns. He happened to notice that several of the more aggressive male dogs slinking past him had bloody butts. He thought at first that it was from fighting. Then he saw what was wrong with them. A good-sized black male came close enough that he could see that he had been castrated, either for fighting or for trying to breed one of the females.

"We will move tomorrow. I will finish this robe by then," she said. "And we can catch up with them. They only want to go a short ways to where the cherries are ripe and pick them."

"Fine." He would ask her about the poor dogs' fate later.

Snow Bear rode his roan horse over and reined him up. "You are coming?"

"Tomorrow. She wants to finish the robe today."

"I see. When we get there you must show me how to use those things." The old man made a sign with his hands. It wasn't apparent to Slocum what he meant, and he frowned at White Swan. She straightened from her work on the hide and said something in Sioux to the man.

"He means the scales they use at the agency," she finally said. "That they weight things on."

"Oh, yes, I will."

"Good. Sometimes I think they tell lies," Snow Bear said.

"No, only the person handling them does that."

Snow Bear shrugged his shoulders. "You can help us."

"I will," he promised.

9

The meadowlarks sang to them and the south wind washed their faces. Slocum rode the dun and White Swan led the sorrel paint. The other packhorses came along, hissing their poles through the short grass and flowers as if on tethers. He offered to let her ride, but she refused. She hadn't worn her leggings and the fringe and buckskin skirt wrapped around her shapely calves.

At midday, they reached a small watercourse. Signs of the tracks of the others were in the stream's muddy edges. Slocum and White Swan ferried the packs over to the other side on his horse so they wouldn't get wet in the crossing; then she drove the other horses across. The animals soon went to grazing, while she nursed the baby and he chewed on some fresh jerky.

Some mallard ducks came flying in. They landed on the water and noisily swam about.

"Be some good eating there," he said, and she agreed.

He took the .30-caliber Colt from his boot and slipped down close. Carefully he picked off two drakes with quick shots before the others took flight. She quickly hoisted her skirt and waded out to retrieve them in the current.

"We should eat them here," she announced, stepping back on the bank and holding her colorful prizes by the neck.

He agreed.

She hurried about gathering wood, which proved scarce since the others had so recently camped there. To assist her, he went and cinched up the dun, and rode upstream to look for some. Pushing the gelding through the dense willows, he concentrated on the search for dry wood, until someone's strong arm swept him from the saddle. He hit the ground hard enough to jar him, and could see the attacker, dressed only in a loincloth, had his knife ready to plunge into him. Lunging Slocum kicked him in the leg and rolled away. His aim was good. The man sprawled facedown where Slocum had been, his knife was stuck in the ground. He roared like an angry grizzly, but by then Slocum was halfway to his feet and ready to face him.

"Today you die, white eyes." Red Hawk jerked the knife out of the ground and charged at him, but the thick willows slowed his movements and Slocum caught his knife hand.

"Not today." Slocum made a pass over his head with the captured wrist, and then around, until he had the man's arm pinned behind his back, then drove him belly-down on the ground.

"Let go of it!" Slocum said through his teeth, and forced the arm higher up Red Hawk's bare back. The warrior never released the hold on the knife, and Slocum strained to shove the arm up further.

"Slocum?" White Swan shouted, and burst through the thick willows.

"I have him," he said through his teeth.

She lashed out with the thick stick in her hands, and delivered a blow to the man's head that was close enough to Slocum's face that he could feel the breeze. The knife fell away as Red Hawk sagged unconscious. Out of breath, Slocum sat up on the man's back.

She held the club high, ready to deliver another blow, but Slocum waved her away. "That's enough."

"If you would kill him, then he would not bother you again."

"I'm more worried about you than me. He wants to marry you." Slocum rubbed his game leg and tried to think of what to do next. He had no plans to murder the man.

Red Hawk started coming to, and groaned. Slocum snatched him by the braids and drew his face close.

"You have no more lives to live. If you ever bother me or her again, I'll kill you. Do you understand?"

Red Hawk's face drew up in anger. The black mask of anger exploded. His fingers sought Slocum's face like claws. When Slocum ducked back, she connected with a full-powered swing of her bat at the back of Red Hawk's head. Pieces of dry wood and bark from the blow showered Slocum's face, and the buck's eyes closed like a curtain.

"Kill him!" she shouted.

Slocum rose to his feet and shook his head. "He has been punished enough today." He gathered the buck's knife, and then went to the man's pony and removed his firearms, an old cap-and-ball pistol and a single-shot .25-20 rifle. She followed along, looking displeased at his refusal to obey her wishes and glancing back at the thicket.

"He is too stupid to ever learn," she muttered.

"Beat to near death by a squaw, he won't dare show his face."

"I can tell you something for sure. He will try to kill you again!"

"He better come early."

"Ha."

Slocum watched the buck slip from the willows, obviously still dazed from her beating. He mounted his horse, rode up the bank, and headed west. Like a slinking coyote, he never paused on the rise. Obviously Red Hawk had had enough for that day. The time would come, Slocum knew, when he would have to settle with this man.

"Next time he will kill you," she said in defiance.

"No," he said, leading the dun by the reins. He had no intention of letting that happen. "Why don't you cook those ducks?"

She dropped her chin as they walked along. "I will, but I will also worry what he does to you next."

He put his arm on her shoulder, leaned close, and kissed her cheek. "I want to eat duck, and then maybe after that we could unroll my bedroll."

She looked at him hard. Then her face melted. "We may never get to Wounded Knee."

"I am not worried about that agent McFaye."

"Good. We will catch the others tomorrow."

"Or the next day. Hmm?"

"Maybe," she said with a look of mischief. Her head thrown back and her braids dancing on her shoulders, she headed for the spot where the fire was smoldering.

She packed the ducks in mud and soon buried them in the hot ashes. He unsaddled the dun and spread out his bedroll in the shade of the gnarled cottonwoods. A strong wind rustled the leaves noisily overhead, and in the upper reaches of the tree, a loud mockingbird mimicked several other birds. Slocum stretched out on his back and flexed his tender leg. He'd be pleased when it was completely well.

She hung the papoose on the tree and busied herself doing beadwork on some deerskin.

"Someday, I'll need to leave you," he said.

She nodded and busied herself. "You have no home?"

"No. Some fella wanted me to come to Montana on a cattle deal. He's probably found someone else by now."

He didn't want to have to explain to her how he had been at loose ends since the end of the war. He had no place to go home to. His parents and brother dead, he had left the family farm in Georgia after killing a carpetbagger judge. Then, in a Kansas-Missouri border town festering with anti-Southern sentiment, he had been forced into a gunfight. He had been hounded ever since by bounty men and full-time tracker deputies, the Abbott brothers. His home now was where his Stetson found a hook or his horse grabbed a blade of grass. The father of the foolish young man who'd died in the gunfight that day owned the law in Ft. Scott, Kansas. His pockets were bottomless for the revenge he sought. Sooner or later someone would show up and try to collect the bounty; they always did, wherever Slocum was. The Sioux reservation would be no safer than anywhere else.

"You look so serious," she said, and lowered herself to lie beside him, breaking his thoughts.

With a smile of approval he turned to face her. She quickly

shucked her skirt and kicked it away with her flashing brown legs. He knew now why she had not put on her leggings. The notion made him want to laugh, but he contained it and drew her face by the chin to his mouth. She threw her arm over him and their lips melted together. His eye lids closed out the bright sun, and the rush of the stream disappeared from his ringing ears.

Fingers fumbled with his belt buckle, his buttons, and shoved away galluses. They pushed down his pants and underwear, until at last the hard pole of his manhood was swept by the hard wind. Her fingertips explored the ring and the tight head. She inspected and traced the veins that bulged blue under the surface. Then, as if satisfied with her inspection, she settled on her back and whispered her readiness.

He rose on his knees and moved between her silky legs. The breeze ruffled his hair, and he stripped off the vest and shirt, letting her squirm a little impatiently. At last, as the wind swept his back and bare butt, he lowered himself, and anticipation glinted in her eyes. He guided the probe in her wet gates, and then settled into the waves of pleasure as he inched deeper and deeper into her fiery trap.

Her muscles in the circle of fire began to spasm and contract. Soon he found himself hopelessly bound in the wedge of her power, being stripped by the tight noose inside her womb. His thrusts were labored and wild with his unbridled need. Her legs pointed skyward on both sides of him as she hunched hard underneath him.

Twice, she half fainted in pleasure, and quickly she returned to the fury of his pumping. Their pubic bones smashed together in search of some relief. At last the forces of passion crushed his testicles and the red-hot molten lava flowed from them, up the stem, and exploded out the head.

He stayed pressed hard into the depth of her, and let the strength evaporate from the cramped muscles of his butt. At last, they wilted, still connected as one, lay down on their sides, and savored the peace that swept over them. He looked deep into her brown eyes and wondered how he would ever be able to leave this woman.

· · ·

The following dawn, the horses were loaded and they were on the move, determined to catch up with the others. He rode the dun and stretched, talking absently to the papoose hung on the saddle horn, while she led the lead travois horse. The other horses obediently came across the rolling grassland behind it.

He wouldn't try to talk her out of walking, even though he could lead the mare and she could ride with him. When she walked along, she felt in charge of her train, and that was where she belonged when moving. They scattered meadowlarks in their wake, and a few blue grouse even flushed at their approach.

Ravens called and flew over in great glides to inspect them. Slocum wondered about Red Hawk. Had he gone back to the main camp and explained the loss of his firearms? Perhaps she was right, the only answer was kill the man. Maybe he had no sense. But Slocum shrugged away the notion. He tried not to kill anyone whenever possible. Life was too precious to be wasted.

He inhaled the smell of cedar and sage. The wind threatened his hat, and out of habit he turned his head so the Stetson remained in place. The sun glistened off the waving blades of grass that rolled like ocean waves in the stiff breeze. Then the sight of tepees and campfire smoke came into view. They had caught up with the village, and dogs began to herald their coming.

"Why did they cut so many dogs back there?" he asked her as they started down the steep grade.

"The women were mad that day for having to move so soon, and took their wrath out on the dogs who were being so aggravating."

"Man, you ever get that mad at me, tell me and I'll leave."

She looked up at him, and then shook her head. "Now I have my bluff in. That is the word to use, isn't it?"

"Yes," he said, and threw his leg over the horn and dismounted to walk with her.

"I will be the most powerful woman in camp."

They both laughed aloud. They sauntered down the grade, and he felt at ease. More so than he had felt in many years.

10

Kicking Dog came to join him while the women assisted White Swan in putting up her tepee. When the poles stood in place, they drew up the skins hand-over-hand on the rope. Others tossed the tepee's covering around so the wrinkles came out and the sides hung like they should. Once the skins were in place, and the older women had argued whether it all was satisfactory or not, they began tying it all down on the stakes driven in the ground.

"Some of my men want to join the wild ones," Kicking Dog said.

"Are you surprised?"

"No. I came here from Ft. Robinson after Red Cloud said this would be Lakota land forever. He told me the treaty said we could hunt and raise horses on this land. It had much grass and there were still many *wetonkas* here then.

"Others stayed at the fort, but I had no wish to be a post Indian. I brought my people to this land and we have not bothered the whites, though they came on the reservation and slaughtered the *wetonka* for their hides. Now this man McFaye says I must be a post Indian. I must stand like a squaw and hold out my hand for his mealy food."

"How long can the others stay out there?" Slocum asked, indicating the west.

"I do not know. Someday the Lakota that are left will all

be put in a small chicken pen like I saw one time. Scratching in the shit for our food and crowing at dawn. These are bad times to be a chief."

Slocum silently agreed, and watched the women carry White Swan's packs to the tepee while others turned loose her piebald horses. The freed ponies rolled gratefully in the buffalo grass, and made dust by squirming on their backs to scratch themselves. Soon they rose, shook off the dirt, and moved away to graze with his dun.

"Snow Bear cannot forget those Blackfeet camps," Kicking Dog said.

"It was not a good sign."

"He says that the wild ones will end like that too."

"I'm no witch to see ahead, but time could bring that. Your allies, the Cheyenne, were driven from Kansas. The Arapahoes were forced from Colorado."

"Will we lose this land?"

"Is there gold here?"

Kicking Dog nodded. He understood what Slocum meant. The chief knew the Lakotas' Black Hills were filled with miners and boomtowns. A place so sacred his people never even camped in the interior was being desecrated by several thousand prospectors, usurping the clear waters and killing the trout with their greedy ways.

"If I found any gold here, I would bury it so deep they would never find it," Kicking Dog said.

Slocum nodded. That would be the best thing the man could do. Except it never worked.

"Some of the young men will leave before we reach the agency," the chief said.

"I know how you have tried to avoid this, and I can offer you nothing but my sadness for your loss."

"This man wishes us to be counted. Does he forget how many we are each time after he does it?"

"Maybe. No, he is only a flunky for a man in Washington, D.C."

"The Great Chief?"

"No, lower than that. The Great Chief only hears the big things or the bad things."

"He did not send this one?" Kicking Dog blinked as if he did not understand this.

"A man lower than the Great Chief sent McFaye."

"I cannot understand how they could send such a man."

"They have worse ones to send."

"Worse?" Kicking Dog frowned in disbelief.

"Much worse."

"Will they come next?"

"I hope not."

"I will remember that. You say they have worse ones than this one to send to us. I will share that with Snow Bear." Kicking Bear looked as if he couldn't possibly stand a worse agent than McFaye.

"Tell these young men to worry about their wives and children before they leave the reservation. If they run for the wild ones, and they make war with the soldiers, the lead bullets will find their dear ones too."

"That is why I came here. I am not afraid to die. But my heart would ache if the children were killed. Even one of them."

"You have done the right thing," Slocum said.

"I have asked the Spirit Woman to come and tell me what to do. But all I hear is the empty wind."

"Perhaps she has no answer." Slocum tossed up small handfuls of grass to test the strong breeze.

"Perhaps. Did Red Hawk attack you?"

"How did you know?"

"He said the white soldiers beat him up for no reason and took his guns while he was hunting."

"White Swan hit him in the head several times with a stick. I took his guns and knife. Do you wish them back?"

"No. Too bad she didn't kill him. I would not miss him if he leaves, but he has two wives and many children to feed. They would not follow him."

"Is he one of the troublemakers?"

"Yes, he roused the others today with his false story."

"How many will leave?"

"The young men, maybe ten."

"They are the backbone of the men in your camp."

"Yes, and I would miss them."

"If I can help—whatever you need," Slocum offered.

"I know. Thanks for your words. You are a strange man. First time I saw you, I said this man has no fear. Then, after you talked the army into ten days, I saw you had no fear because you know so many things."

Slocum tried to dismiss the man's praise. But Kicking Dog was not to be dissuaded. The chief rose to his feet and started across the campgrounds for his own great lodge.

Seated by himself on the ground at the tepee entrance, Slocum watched the squaws bringing in more logs, even towing the larger ones with horses. There would be another council, perhaps a stomp dance too, so the people could forget their concerns about what living close to the agency would be like. Slocum had never thought about the obedient-acting women of the tribe being so upset by the order to move as to take their anger out on the aggravating male dogs. The notion still left him stunned.

White Swan brought him a dish of meat and red berries. The tart sweetness drew the saliva in his mouth and he complimented her.

"Kicking Dog came to see you?" she asked.

"He worries about the young men riding off to join the wild ones in the west."

"Are many planning to leave?"

"Ten or so. He's upset about losing them."

"It will be hard to keep them here. They have never had the chance to follow the trail of a warrior. They fear they will never get to do it if they go to this agency."

"You can die anywhere," he said.

"You were not raised a Sioux."

"No," he said. "I was born a Southerner. I went to war too. It was a war we could not ever win. We believed, oh, God, we believed that right was stronger than might and those filthy Northern bastards with their industry and superior ways would never make us submit to their ideas. That we would never let them destroy our beautiful homes, families, and things. But they did, and we lost it all. Our land, cities, fine homes, rich farms, fancy horses. When they were finished, our land looked much like the empty Blackfeet villages." He dropped his chin. "No, I was never a Sioux, but I know how futile war is to solve your differences."

"Futile?" She frowned at the meaning of the word.

"Means worthless. Means it won't work, there is always a stronger army."

"So what can Kicking Dog do?"

"Be the leader. It is easier to die sometimes than to live."

"Did you ever wish to die?"

"Never for very long."

"Have you heard about Red Hawk's lies?"

He nodded and rose to stand with her.

"We should have killed him," she said with a frown.

"Hell, you tried." Then he reached out and hugged her. "The days ahead will be troubled," he said to the top of her head, looking at the straight part in her shiny black hair.

Her arms encircled him and they hugged each other for a long while. He watched another squaw drag a dead snag past for the council fire.

The sun set fiery red over the distant Black Hills. Snow Bear came and invited Slocum to join the council.

"But this is Sioux business," Slocum replied.

"Come. We need many wise heads to talk of the future."

"Will it convince anyone?" Slocum asked, rising to his feet.

Snow Bear paused and smiled. The older man seldom did that. His sun-wrinkled leathery face always bore a solemn look. "Kicking Dog said you would know the outcome before you left your tepee. I hoped that with talk we could convince the younger ones to stay. But I know if we tied them hand and foot, some would still escape and join the wild ones."

"I will come if my presence does not rile the men."

"You are our brother, no longer a white man, but a brother."

Slocum wanted to tell him differently, that many would always consider him an outsider even if he lived there forever. He decided to please Snow Bear and Kicking Dog and go to their council.

With a nod to White Swan, he followed Snow Bear across

the campground in the twilight to the center of the camp, where the flames of the fire licked the sky. He took a place next to the older man on a robe, and nodded to the others around him.

Slocum could see the eagerness in the younger men. They acted ready to take flight. An impatience shone in their eyes; it would be hard to talk them out of leaving. He settled back, at first refusing the food offered to him, then sampling some of it to fit in. He listened to the first speaker, and listened to Snow Bear's short translations.

"Our brothers in the west are strong. They number in the thousands—with new rifles and ammunition. If we are men, then we should join them, help them defend our lands, our game, the *wetonka*—"

"They have a vision—" Slocum listened as the speeches favoring joining the wild ones continued. Their brothers were out there. Enough numbers to turn the blue coats away and send the rest back where they came from. The Sioux must take a stand. Strong words. Words of defiance. How the Great Spirit was with the wild ones and had abandoned the reservation Lakotas.

Slocum expected such oratory from them. He'd heard the same things over a decade earlier in the Confederate Army, only then it was secession and states' rights. Then it was "the cause" that would win their war. They were in the right and they knew it.

Finally, it became Snow Bear's time to speak, and Slocum listened to the guttural words. Though he did not know their meaning, he knew the man spoke of their ancient enemy, the Blackfeet, and the ghost villages. How the ancient enemy had once spread over the land like blades of grass because there were so many of them. Now there were a only a handful of them left in Montana. Gone were the wonderful herds of ponies in their paint colors and striking piebalds. Their ghost camps lay silent and empty. Then Snow Bear called on Brown Badger to tell them more of what they saw in the north.

The young man stood up and nodded in agreement with Snow Bear's words. His heart was not in leaving. Slocum heard it in his words. But still, their speech did not persuade many of the other men.

"I would rather die as a Lakota warrior than die as a white man's dog," one of them said sharply in English to Slocum.

Slocum nodded, then started to rise, and Kicking Dog made a sign with his hands for him to stand and talk.

"I am not a Lakota," Slocum said. "I am your guest. I speak because I once went to war for what I believed. Look at me. I have lost my land, my family, my way of life. Go to war like a blind angry dog and get killed. Then you won't hear your children cry for food and shelter when the snow comes. It is easy to ride off and let the women and children suffer in the cold. Why will you care? You will be with the Great Spirit. You will be a hero." He paused, and the buzzing of translations and private whispering went round the circle. A large log crashed in the fire, and sparks flew ten feet high.

"It will take a bigger man to stay and help his people find a new way," he said.

His face filled with rage, one of the younger ones rose to his feet, shaking his fist at Slocum and shouting in Sioux.

"He says you lie for the agent," Snow Bear said from where he sat.

Slocum shook his head in disbelief. "That man needs no one to lie for him. He can do enough himself." The words and translation brought many soft laughs and nods of agreement.

"What should they do?" Kicking Dog asked, and motioned for him to remain standing.

"I have said what I think they must do. Learn the new way and then the next new way. It will be easy to die, much easier."

"The wild ones with Sitting Bull won't die, they have magic," a defiant one shouted. "The Great Spirit gave them strong medicine."

"Bullets are magic." Slocum shook his head at the man. "They can kill even the most powerful spirit. The army has many bullets, many guns. They will come like the clouds of grasshoppers do in the moon of the chokecherries and strip the land." He had said enough.

A buck jumped up and stomped his feet. Obviously, he had no fear of grasshoppers. His words in Sioux were more of the same, defiant.

Slocum sat down and the argument raged on. Snow Bear nudged him. "Now it is time that Kicking Dog spoke."

The chief rose and nodded. He spoke, then pointed to the far side of the fire.

"He wants those who wish to join the wild ones to go over there," Snow Bear said softly to Slocum.

The first one jumped up and rushed to the far side. Then others did the same, anger and belligerence written on their copper faces, which shone in the firelight. At last five were there, looking at each other, obviously feeling self-conspicuous.

Kicking Dog asked if there were more. But the others around the fire shook their heads.

"Each man here should give them a bullet apiece," Snow Bear said in his next translation. The chief sent them around to hold out their hands for the offering. Acting self-consciously, the five did as they were told, and Slocum took cartridges from his gunbelt for them.

Then Kicking Dog asked the first one if he was taking his family. The man dropped his head, and after a while shook it. Quickly, he began to offer an explanation for why he was leaving them behind. They would be in danger from the soldiers on the way out there. White men might capture them. Slocum caught enough to understand.

"Who do you give your wife to then?" Kicking Dog asked. "I must know, for she will need to be cared for if you are killed or can't return."

The young buck shook his head. He did not understand what the chief meant. He was not giving his wife to someone else.

Kicking Dog insisted. There would be no coming back to the reservation. The army would not let them. What was his wife to do? Starve?

The buck wilted and went back around the circle, returning the shells. Two others did the same. The last two stood defiantly.

Slocum had no doubt they would go and join the wild ones. Kicking Dog's bold plan had won several back. But how long would his threat work? No telling. The drums began to beat, and the women appeared as if on cue. It would be a late-night stomp.

White Swan came and led him to the circle. He busied himself learning the shuffling gait to the drums and the voices singing, "Ho-yah-ho-yah." It would have been easier in moccasins rather than his boots, but he imitated the others, and soon was dancing around the blazing fire with her. The pride she showed and the look on her face warmed him. He did this for her, so she could show him off. Even the tender leg did not stop his dancing. Besides, it was far better than the arguing.

11

"Red Hawk and three others left last night," Kicking Dog told Slocum the next morning. They stood on the ridge in the strong breath of the morning wind and studied the busy camp below. A ruffled raven tried to balance on a nearby cedar bough, as if eavesdropping on them.

"Did they give their wives away?"

"No."

"Still, that was not as many as you originally thought."

"One was my son, Big Elk."

Slocum nodded.

"He had no wife."

"Would you have gone if you were him?"

Kicking Dog cut his eyes around and glared at Slocum. "Why do you ask such questions? You know the answers."

"Yes, but it's you who must answer them."

"Yes, if I was that young and awoke each morning with a stiff hard dick, if I had no wife, no children, I would have gone too."

"Maybe he will learn what he seeks and come back."

Kicking Dog nodded. "Snow Bear wishes to go one more time to the Paha Sapa."

"He will find many white men all over those hills," Slocum warned him.

"He knows that, but he would like for one more time to

speak to the spirits before they are gone. He wishes for you to take him there."

"Why did he not ask me himself?"

"It is not the way."

"Fine. Tell him we can go there and try to find what he wants to see. But it will be very dangerous. Perhaps with him dressed as a white man we can slip in there. They see an Indian, they're liable to shoot. They're crazy as loons, those prospectors."

"We will speak about this later today. The women wish to pick more berries here. We won't move camp until tomorrow."

"Good," Slocum said, and went off to check on his and White Swan's horses. He liked to be certain they were still with the others in the herd. When he found them grazing under the care of several young boys, he nodded his approval and started back. It would be a much hotter day.

At mid-morning, the two men joined Slocum where he sat in the shade and repaired a sheath for his skinning knife. The lacing was rotten and he was replacing it.

"Before we go to the agency, Snow Bear would like to see the Paha Sapa," Kicking Dog said.

"He would have to go there as a white man. I mean, dressed as one. There are many white men there. They're liable to shoot an Indian."

"Clothes, you mean?" Kicking Dog asked.

"Yes, wear white man's clothing and ride in a white man's saddle on a solid-colored horse. It would still be very dangerous." Slocum looked at the two of them hard; he wanted to set some strict rules before he would participate in this quest.

"I am not afraid of death," Snow Bear said.

"It won't do any good to get killed. You could go by yourself and do that." Slocum hoped his message was clear to them.

Both men agreed with him.

"We thought you could help," the chief said.

"I wish to speak to the Great Spirit Woman for Kicking

Dog," Snow Bear explained. "If she will answer me. Those hills would put me closer to her, and maybe she can hear me from there."

Slocum agreed, but he wondered if she would even be present.

"It will rain in another day and that might hide us," Snow Bear said. "There will be much rain, and then we can go there and not many will see us."

Slocum looked to the skies. They were clear and bright blue. Not a cloud in sight. How did the old man know it would rain? Weather would make a wonderful cover, but he doubted it was about to rain, certainly not enough to cover their trip to the hills and their return. Damn, he hoped their journey went without a hitch. That might be too much to ask.

"I will find the clothes to wear and the saddle," Snow Bear said. Then he looked off as if all was not completed. "A solid-colored horse?"

"Yes. A white man can ride a paint, but they will look hard at anyone on one."

"I will borrow one of those too."

"Good." He would need to tell White Swan of their plans. He dreaded her reaction, though it shouldn't upset her. It was her holy man he was taking up there.

"Borrow a slicker too," Slocum added. It made sense for Snow Bear to have one, even if it was a cloudless sky. He was the one who'd predicted the rain.

"You are going where?" she demanded, standing over him inside the tepee.

Slocum held his hands up. "Snow Bear wants to go to the Paha Sapa one last time before we go to Wounded Knee."

"What for?"

"To speak to the Spirit Woman."

"You are going too?"

"I'm going to help him get there. He's dressing as a white man."

"Stupid thing. It will be like the trip to steal the horses. What can he find? More white men shit-houses?"

"He knows it will be different, but there is nothing I can say."

"Say you aren't going!"

Slocum shook his head. He liked Snow Bear, considered him a good man and a medicine man still with powers. Powers that could heal many things. He also wanted the experience of this trip; witches, priests, all of that fascinated him. Perhaps he too wanted to be touched, but he knew their faith was the real power. No, he could not deny Snow Bear his assistance in what might be his final journey to the once-sacred land.

"Go! Go and get killed." She folded her arms on her blouse over her proud milk-filled breasts. He rose and caught her by the waist. She tried to avoid him by leaning backward.

Soon his mouth was nestled on the soft skin of her neck, kissing, nipping, and teasing her. Her resisting hands weakened, and they soon slipped around his neck. They sank to their knees on the robes, mouth locked on mouth, seeking each other. His right hand undid the laces on the side of her skirt, and he pushed it downward, exposing her long tight ass to his palm. He began to knead it.

She shoved away his vest and galluses, then in a frenzy undid his pants with quick fumbling fingers. Her hand sought him with an urgency, and she pulled on his shaft with a vengeance, making it stiff and hard.

With his pants and underwear shoved down far enough to expose his butt, she moved to lie down and pulled him after her. He settled between her legs, and soon was inside her silken gates, pumping her with his best efforts. She closed her long eyelashes and savored it, hunching with her back for him to go even deeper.

They became wilder, grunting and groaning in the effort to reach the top. He felt the head of his shaft swell so tight, he thought it might burst. Then she began whispering, "Yes, yes."

In a blinding force he managed to come, deep and hard inside her. The force sent rockets off in his brain, and they showered down with red stars. He fell to the robe beside her and closed his eyes. Depleted and exhausted, he lay there and idly played with one of her braids.

"Be very careful on this journey, Slocum," she said softly.
"I will, I will," he promised.

He and Snow Bear mounted their horses in the late afternoon.
Even Snow Bear's felt hat was shaped like a cowboy's; Slocum was taking no chances. They rode west from the camp.
Hoping to make better time, they left in the daylight. All they
needed to do was avoid any army patrols. Slocum felt there
might be some military activity between them and the badlands, which also had to be crossed to reach the hills.

Snow Bear knew the way, and Slocum felt grateful. At
twilight they watered at a spring Slocum would have never
known existed. Snow Bear led them up a blind canyon, and
there under a rock ledge was a clean spring to water them
and their horses. That completed, they rode on.

"When we get up there, we will have to ride the roads
through the towns," Slocum said. "The downed timber is too
thick to try and go across country."

Snow Bear agreed.

Late the next afternoon, the hills came in sight. They
reached a set of wagon tracks that led westward toward them.
Slocum wondered where the man wanted to go, but Snow
Bear had his secret place and Slocum wouldn't ask him. So
they followed the wagon ruts into the foothills.

Thunder in the distance brought a smile to Slocum's lips,
and soon clouds blocked the sky. In a short while rain began
to fall, steady and cold. Both men put on their slickers and
continued. They reached a settlement. Water had begun to fill
the set wagon tracks, and the stream they rode beside had
begun to gurgle in earnest.

"Let's find some shelter and go again come dawn," Slocum
said. With only a few hours of sleep the night before, he felt
weary.

"Good idea," Snow Bear said over the rain.

They managed to discover some empty sheds. Slocum
lighted a match and found the first one fairly dry, with no
sign of recent inhabitants, and he led his dun inside under the
shake roof. The cow pony shook to rid himself of the rain
until the stirrups popped. Slocum tied him and listened. He

could hear further up the canyon, over the drip and splash of the rain, a squeeze-box accordion playing and the noise of folks having fun.

"What is it?" Snow Bear asked softly, motioning toward the music.

"White men having a stomp. I may go see and ask about this road and where it leads."

Snow Bear nodded. "I'll stay here and watch the horses."

"Yeah, it'll be best."

He left the shed, and the long yellow slicker wrapped itself around his legs in the steady rain. On the mountain above, a streak of lightning struck a tree and decapitated it in a blinding bolt that shook the ground under his soles.

His toes soon squished with water in his boots as he sloshed along. When he reached the saloon porch, he paused to look over the bat-wing doors, and seeing a huge woman seated on the bar, pushed his way in. His entrance drew a few looks from the men who were crowded around to see the show.

She had her huge bare butt and both of her feet on the bar with her knees spread wide apart. Her bare legs looked like great white hams of a hog, a giant one at that. And the miners were staring at her exposed pubic area, fringed in woolly-looking black hair.

"It's the mother lode, boys," she said, and laughed. Her numerous chins vibrated with her hilarity, and her small red eyes soon picked out Slocum.

"Hey, stranger, get over here, I want to show you mine."

"I've seen mines before," he said, and stood at the bar down the way.

She swung her butt around and bared herself to him. Her actions drew loud shouts and catcalls from the onlookers.

"What'll it be, pussy or whiskey?" the barkeep asked with a suppressed laugh.

"Double rye. It's been wet out there." Slocum glanced over when she turned back to the others. The crowd shouted and laughed at her antics.

"It's a mother lode," she said to Slocum over her shoulder.

"No offense, ma'am, I'll take mine in gold." He touched

his hat to her and slapped down a silver dollar to pay the barkeep.

"I say there ain't a man-jack among you can plug this hole," she challenged them.

"Mister, she's talking to you," a bearded man in overalls said to Slocum.

"No, she's you boys' delight. I'm just passing through."

"All right, he don't want to play," she sneered. "You there, boy, you got you a hard-on there," she said to one of the onlookers. "Get up on that chair and see if you can stick it in me."

A chair scraped on the floor, and the young man was assisted to stand on it. He dropped his galluses, and his bare white hatchet butt soon shone under the lamplight. She scooted close to the edge and caught him by the neck. Then she shoved his face downward, and the others quickly held him by the arms, pressing him forward.

"Lick it! Lick it!" she screamed, and the crowd laughed aloud.

"This road take me to Deadwood?" Slocum asked the bartender over the shouting and hooting.

"Yeah, take the right fork up here a mile or so."

"This go on every night?" Slocum asked him, nodding toward the woman.

"Naw, Sadie just got here this week. Sure sells lots of whiskey, and she'll screw a dozen of them before the night's over. My part's two bucks a head," the man said loud enough for Slocum to hear over the cheers and cussing.

The deal looked like a free-for-all to him.

"That's enough," she said, and with a great fat hand on the boy's neck, she jerked him upright. "Now put that pole of yours in me. You get a free one."

The youth would have fallen off the chair, but they steadied him. She hugged him and pulled him tight to her mountainous breasts while the unsteady boy, standing on the chair, aimed his rod for her target.

Slocum had had enough. Even the whiskey tasted flat. He started for the door.

"Hey, big man, he's about to come already. There, he

came! You're next!" she bellowed at Slocum's back, and the men's laughter followed him out the swinging doors.

Rain drilled down on his hat and slicker in the inky night. Slocum paused, listening for any pursuit. But after a short while, he decided that they must have all stayed for her show.

"You learn much up there?" Snow Bear asked when he returned. He was looking over Slocum's shoulder for anyone following him.

"Yeah, the right fork goes to Deadwood. And they have the biggest whore up there I have ever seen. She must weigh over three hundred pounds plus. Bigger than a grizzly bear."

They both laughed. Slocum got out a blanket. He aimed to get some sleep. The drum of rain on the roof might let him. He hoped so. They had another day of rain to face if he believed Snow Bear's forecast.

12

The rain held. The thunder's repeated roar rolled up and down the canyon. Low clouds passed through the dark timber on the steep slopes. Despite their rain gear, Slocum and Snow Bear felt like two drown rats as they pushed their horses up the wagon road.

They rode in silence past the saloon. It looked deserted and dark. One sodden drunk lay passed out on the leaking porch, and a blue tick hound was curled up close to him for the warmth. He never barked at their passage. Where they crossed the creek, the murky water had grown deeper from the runoff. It was not the time of year for a sudden flood, but if the deluge kept up, Slocum knew the sheer rocky peaks would shed the water fast enough to make for some hellacious flooding.

Hours later it was still raining when they reached a pass with an open alpine-like meadow. They paused to stand under some dripping pines and let the horses graze through their bits on the grass. Slocum offered Snow Bear some of White Snow's jerky, but the man refused, and busied himself studying the peaks that were occasionally visible in the storm.

"We still going the right way?" Slocum asked, and Snow Bear agreed while still absorbed in his own thoughts.

"We'll be in Deadwood by dark." Slocum waited for Snow Bear's reply.

No answer.

After the horses had taken their fill, Slocum retightened his cinch and nodded to the man. Snow Bear bobbed his head, still preoccupied with something, and they headed for Deadwood. The rain continued. Thunder rolled over the mountains, and Slocum became more concerned about the deepening streams they crossed.

They reached a small hamlet wedged in a canyon. Miners driven to cover peered at them from under porches and out of open doorways. Slocum dismounted at a store and went inside the dark interior. He bought some cigars and lucifer matches that he had the clerk wrap in oilcloth. Then, with a small sack of hard candy, he went out, mounted the dun, and they proceeded.

Further on, they found a freight wagon spilled on its side, the contents dumped in the creek. Two men, up to their waists, were straining to recover boxes from the boulder-strewn water and trying to get them on the bank.

"Hey, we'd pay you good to help us," one shouted in an Irish brogue.

Slocum shook his head. He couldn't risk exposing Snow Bear's identity no matter how much he felt for the men in their plight.

They rode past a large draft horse still in harness that lay dead on his side, no doubt destroyed for a broken leg that had happened in the wreck. Another soaked horse in harness stood nearby tied to a pine. It had been a big loss for the freighters, but Slocum felt he and Snow Bear needed to ride on, despite the men calling after him.

Every inch of Slocum was wet or clammy. His hat was so sodden, it felt like a great block on his head. The brim bobbed, and rain guttered off it in a stream. His feet had been wet so long, they had little feeling left in his boots. He was worried that they were so soaked the leather would soon fall apart. If he pulled them off, he knew he would never get them on again. The two men pushed on to Deadwood.

"We need to find us a room and dry out," he said to Snow Bear over the wind that lashed them with more rain.

Snow Bear surrendered with a nod.

"I'll find us a place where they don't ask questions," Slocum said.

They entered Deadwood, and he spotted a soiled dove standing in the doorway of a narrow crib house. She was a large-framed woman, and appeared to be in pain as she huddled in a blanket on the lookout for business. Slocum held a hand out and made Snow Bear stop. He booted the dun over and looked up and down the street. Nothing but wagons moving. Everyone else was under cover. Thunder rolled over head, and she looked apprehensively at the sky.

"Business slow?" he asked.

She frowned at him. "Damn rain's got them all run off." From her accent she was European, maybe German. And a lot younger than he'd originally thought. Still, she looked like his best bet.

"That old man won't hurt you. All we need to do is dry out and change our clothes and get some sleep."

"Who is he?"

"He's just an old man. I'm prepared to pay you five dollars to stay in there until dawn." He motioned toward her crib.

"I got to do both of you for that?" She curled her thin lip in displeasure.

"No, we just want a dry place to sleep for the night." He scowled at the continuing rain. It was past being even interesting. And this woman wouldn't earn what he'd offered to pay her in two good nights. What was she so damn fussy about anyway?

"They got boardinghouses for that."

"You want five dollars or not?"

"Sure. Don't talk so tough. What's his name?" She nodded her head at Snow Bear and drew the blanket around her tighter.

"Bear."

"Mr. Bear," she called out to him. "Come on inside. It's cold and nasty out here."

Slocum looked at the darkening sky for help. Mr. Bear. Oh, hell, what a fix. He dismounted, looking around to be certain they didn't attract any more attention than necessary.

Snow Bear started inside and removed his wet hat. She sucked in her breath. "He's an Indian!"

"A tame one. Now take it easy. He won't hurt you. That's why I am paying you five dollars. Now be quiet and quit fidgeting."

"All right, all right," she said, but he could she was visibly shaken. She dropped on her butt to sit on the bed, and made a perplexed face at Snow Bear.

Slocum took off the man's slicker, and motioned for him to sit on a chair in the narrow room. Snow Bear looked tired, his leathery face drawn and his eyelids heavy.

"Now I'm going up the street to the livery and put up our horses," Slocum said to the woman. "Can you get us some food, or can I get some on the way back?"

"Chinese place a ways this side of the stables," she said with her round shoulders trembling from standing so long in the cold.

"You ate?"

"No-o-o," she managed, still looking at the floor.

"What's your name?"

"Greta."

"Greta, he is just a tired old man. Stop worrying."

"But-but I've never been this close to an—Indian before."

"Stop worrying." He looked at Snow Bear and scowled. "Say something in English to her. She thinks you're a ghost."

"Where is a place to go?" He looked around anxiously.

"I have a pot under the bed," she said, and reached for it. Snow Bear nodded to her. They were communicating anyway.

"Good," Slocum said. "You two get along. I'm going to put the horses up and get us some food."

He hunched his shoulders, rebuttoned his rubber slicker, and stepped outside in the hard-blowing rain. Bent over against it, he mounted the dun and led Snow Bear's horse after him. The street had turned to a quagmire, and up and down it wagons were stuck. Mud sucked at his horses' hooves until at last he reached the stable on the hillside between two saloons. A tinny piano was playing in one of them, and it sounded like a happy place from the noise and laughter. He dismounted and led the ponies inside the stable's hallway. The deep sour-sweetness of horse manure crowded his nose.

"Two bits a night paid in advance." The whiskered stable man held the lantern up to shine in his face.

"I've got the money." Slocum dug in his pocket. "I'll be after them at first light," he said, paying him.

"You've got till ten o'clock. Then you owe me for another day."

"I'll beat that."

"Suit yourself. If it don't quit this damn raining, you may stay longer."

Even the sanctuary of the smelly stable felt good after being rained on all night and day. He slipped outside and made for the saloon porch next door. With a scramble up the steep steps, he was under the roof and could look inside. The place was filled with cigar smoke and gamblers playing cards. It was warm and inviting, but he pushed past the barker at the door advertising the availability of plump ladies and cheap whiskey inside.

Ducking and darting in and out of the rain from porch to porch, he finally made it to the Chinese restaurant. The sharp aroma of ginger assailed his senses when he went inside. After much talking, the small Oriental woman told him that she would fill a large iron kettle full of meat, rice, and vegetables for one dollar, but he must bring back her kettle.

"What kind of meat?" he asked her, wondering if she would understand.

"Beef—all beef cows!"

"Good." He didn't eat dog with the Sioux. He wasn't eating cats with the Chinese. Then he smiled to himself. As scarce and high-priced as cats were on the frontier, beef was probably a lot cheaper and easier to get.

He managed to talk her into lending him three large spoons too. Kettle handle in hand, he started for Greta's with the woman saying, "You bring back, you bring back."

"I promise, lady, I will or Greta will. You know Greta? Good."

His sole slipped in the mud crossing the side street in the rain, but he didn't go down, and reached the next boardwalk with his boots turned into large gobs of mud. The windswept rain washed his face as he strode down the boardwalk.

At last at Greta's door, he knocked, and she was long in answering. Then she looked around in the storming night, and at last she swung the door open for him to enter. He saw Snow Bear in his loincloth, sitting on the edge of the bed. His clothes were hanging to dry on a line she had put up that stretched across the narrow room. Obviously, from the welcome warmth that struck Slocum's face, she had a fire going in the small stove.

"Got a bucket of food," he said, holding up the kettle.

"Good," she said, acting strange.

He tried to ignore it. "Got food," he said to Snow Bear, who nodded at the sight of the kettle.

She pulled out a chest to put it on in front of Snow Bear, then drew the straight-back chair up for Slocum. She found a small crate for herself to sit upon. Slocum stripped off the slicker and set his wet hat aside. Grateful to be inside and warm at last, he drew a deep breath. It had been a long two days, and the dry confines of her narrow crib, filled with the smell of perfume, were a welcome haven. Maybe at last he would dry out some.

They ate from the kettle. Snow Bear said little. Greta made small talk about how badly the rain had hurt her business. The panners couldn't work the flooded creeks, so the free gold was getting scarce. Then the panners got stingy with it, afraid they wouldn't find any more. Miners got paid on Saturday, but she relied on the prospectors for her clients. The miners got drunk, and ended up being bedded in the saloons before they came out broke.

Oh, she got some innocent ones. Inexperienced kids, she called them, afraid of going in saloons for fear they'd get robbed.

"How did you get to Deadwood?" Slocum asked her when he finished eating and dug out a cigar. Full of the stew, he watched Snow Bear, still bending over and shoveling in the spicy mixture. Then Slocum lighted the cigar and drew deep, the nicotine settling him.

"I come to this country to marry Hans Broeken," she said.

"He sent me my passage and money to come to Minnesota. So I come with my dowry in my trunk, only I don't know that Hans, he is not going to marry me. All is a big lie about him marrying me. He takes me to this lumber camp and them loggers, they undressed me of all my clothes, hold me down, and stick it in me." She straightened her shoulders under the white shift she wore. "Some way to lose your virgin business, huh? Must have been thirty of them that night did it to me.

"Hans says, now, Greta, you see what you must do in America. You can be nice and fuck men for me, or I will take you back to that log camp for another lesson."

Slocum blew out smoke at the ceiling. "Not much choice."

"So I say, why do it for Hans and give him all the money? So one day I tell this freighter who comes by for me for him to take me to Deadwood where the gold is and I will sleep with him on the way. I can cook too. So he brought me here and I rented this place. Don't work for Hans or no one."

"I see," he said, looking up when Snow Bear belched out loud. "Better?" Slocum asked him. He nodded.

She talked on about Germany and where she'd lived. How it looked like Deadwood, which was much better than Minnesota. Slocum finished his cigar, put on his slicker, went out, and used the outhouse. Rain sloshed at the small frame structure, and drips from the leaky roof fell on his head. He would be glad when this whole ordeal was over. When he returned, she was busy stoking the small coal stove, and the heat from it quickly drove out the chill from his damp clothing.

"Where will you sleep?" she asked.

"Floor will do me," Slocum said, looking around the narrow room. There wasn't much room besides the cot.

"We can put the cot up and all sleep down there," she said. "Or else someone won't have a place to lay down."

"Fine," he said. The carpeted floor would be all right.

So he helped her fold the cot, and she spread a blanket on the floor. Snow Bear said nothing, but stayed back until she pointed for him to lie down. He nodded, and soon lay on his side. She blew out the lamp and quickly took a place between them. Bone tired and soothed by the room's warmth, Slocum soon found himself in deep sleep.

He awoke to someone's loud nasal grunting. He frowned in the darkness. The lightning illuminated the room enough for him to see Snow Bear was on top of her, pumping away. Thunder rolled over the small crib, made the thin walls of the shack vibrate, then rumbled off down the canyon. Slocum shrugged, drew a deep breath, and went back to sleep.

At dawn, he dressed, and hurried Snow Bear to get his clothes on. It was still raining, and the street out in front had turned into a river. The creek behind them was a raging torrent, and he wanted out of there.

When they were ready to leave, he paid her, and she nodded in thanks. "Still raining. You could stay longer for less."

"No, we have business."

Snow Bear agreed. He acted anxious to be on his way. When they were outside on the boardwalk, thunder rolled close overhead and they both ducked. Slocum decided no one could see who Snow Bear was. Just another wet fool in a slicker out in the storm. They hurried to the livery, saddled in the dimly lit barn, mounted up, and rode out into the knee-deep flood coming down the street. Snow Bear took the lead, and they pushed up the mountain. In a few hours, he led them to a dry cave that was big enough to house even their horses.

Rain fell in curtains outside. Someone had left some rusty cooking utensils and even firewood inside. Snow Bear opened his bedroll, spread it out, and drew out his beaded buckskins and great eagle-feather headdress.

Slocum found a comfortable place and sat down to watch. Dressed in his Indian garb, the old man began to make a fire with a small bow and tiny tinder. Soon his fire was burning, and he had handfuls of sage smoke to purify himself with. He used it like water to go over his body.

Then Snow Bear faced the four directions and sent smoke toward them. He worked hard, and sweat ran down his face. Soon he began to chant and stomp-dance. The words were all in his language. The dancing went on for hours. Slocum sat still lest he break the spell.

At last, Snow Bear collapsed to his knees in exhaustion and mopped his wet brow. If he wanted to say something, Slocum gave the man the opportunity. There were no words, so Slocum brought him his bedroll to spread on the floor of the cave. In a short while, the old man fell sound asleep from exhaustion. Slocum went to the entrance and looked over the dark pines and the gentle rain that wept on the forested slopes of the Black Hills.

He lighted a cigar and drew on it. He wondered what White Swan was doing out on the prairie. Nursing the papoose probably, and looking at the horizon for his return. *I am coming home to you. I hope you can hear me. When this old man finishes his business, we will ride swiftly home.*

The wind switched and sprayed a mist in his face. *Soon, White Swan, soon.*

13

"Did the Great Spirit come to talk to you?" Slocum asked Snow Bear.

The man half sat up and shook his head. He looked off at the sun shining in the cave entrance, then numbly shook his head in disappointment. "She must have left the Paha Sapa. She never answered me. Maybe I should not have done that last night with that white woman. Perhaps she was mad because I did that."

"I don't know," Slocum said.

Snow Bear grinned. "She wasn't any different than a Lakota woman."

"Did you think she would be?"

"I always heard things were different down there on a white woman." Snow Bear shook his head and grinned. "Felt the very same anyway." Then he laughed, rose to his knees, and clapped Slocum on the shoulder. "You worked hard to get me here. You are like a brother to me, only more so. I knew you could get me here. But all the way riding here I was afraid the Spirit Woman was gone." He shook his head warily and stood up. "All these white people. They even camped in here, probably even shit in here like dogs would do, in a sacred place. I don't blame her for leaving. She thought all the Lakota forgot her and they sent white men to use this cave for a piss pot like that woman kept under the bed."

"Chamber pot," Slocum said.

"Yeah, that thing. How will we go home?"

"Closest way is to ride back through them."

"You are the guide."

"I don't know about that," Slocum said, and drew up the cinch.

When they reached Deadwood, the rain was only a fine mist. They detoured around collapsed porches, with their underpinnings washed out. Several men were straining to put detached steps back on another porch. The water in the street was going down, but had deposited piles of brown bottles in places.

Greta was nowhere in sight when they passed her crib. The creek still roared and sloshed over the hollow bridge they crossed. Headed east at last, Slocum nodded to Snow Bear, grateful that no one had called out or recognized them. In the meadow again, they only paused a short while to let the horses graze. It grew late in the soggy day. Slocum wanted to make the settlement where they'd stayed in the empty shed the first night in the hills.

They made their way down the canyon in the darkness, trusting their horses' sense more than anything to stay on the road and find the easiest crossing of the gurgling streams they encountered. Before they went many miles, the pitch-dark drizzling night engulfed them, and Slocum began to wish they had found a place earlier to stop. He could hardly see his hand in front of his face. Then he heard the accordion music over the light pitter-pat on his slicker. Good, they were close.

Soon the lights of the saloon could be seen, and he could make out the line of several hip-shot horses tied at the rack in front. Maybe he would stop, have a drink of whiskey, and buy a few cigars for later. The notion of some whiskey to heat up his innards made him agree that he could stand to put up with the huge orgy on the bar one more time.

His dun snorted wearily and he reined him up. The yellow lamplight shone on the last horse at the hitch rail. A familiar tall Appaloosa with a blanket butt. He reined the dun aside toward the opposite side of the road, booted him on, and pulled down the brim on his hat. No mistaking that gelding.

He belonged to Bourbon County, Kansas, Deputy Sheriff Lyle Abbott.

"You not going in?" Bear asked, catching up.

"Not tonight. Not tonight, Snow Bear."

"Bad spirits in there?" the man asked, twisting in the saddle to look back.

"For me, yes. Did you see that Nez Percé horse?"

"Big one?"

"That's what he rides."

"He's someone looking for you?"

"All the time, Snow Bear."

"We could go back and kill him."

"Wouldn't do any good. Besides, I know him on sight and can avoid him. I wouldn't know the next ones."

"Man has enemies, he needs to know them. Those other bastards will sneak up you." Snow Bear turned to look back again, then settled in the saddle as they rode on into the inky night.

Slocum hoped they could make out the sheds. The dun must have recalled the shelter, for he turned and went toward them. Slocum dropped heavily from the saddle and fumbled around to find the door latch. He swung it back and led the dun inside.

"You coming, Snow Bear?"

"Take my horse. I want to go back and see what this man looks like who looks for you."

"Lyle has a brother named Ferd. He's probably with him. Big man, black beard, loud voice."

"I'll be back. You get some sleep." He handed Slocum the reins and hurried off.

Slocum watched the shiny wet slicker disappear. He was concerned for the man's safety prowling around up there, but decided Snow Bear was old enough to know what he wanted to do, so he loosened the old man's cinch. He decided to leave their horses saddled, in case they were forced to flee. Obviously, the notion of his pursuers had aroused Snow Bear's curiosity. Slocum hoped it turned out all right.

•   •   •

Slocum dozed some in his blankets in a dry corner. The horses' snort awoke him, and he hefted the Colt from his lap. He could see by the outline of the hat that it was only Snow Bear.

"Learn anything?"

"Yes. I saw the big woman you mentioned," Snow Bear replied, sounding perplexed.

"And?"

"She is the biggest woman I ever saw. Had legs big as my body."

"Was she showing off?"

"Yes."

"What did you think about that white woman?"

"Way too big for me. You would need a horse's dick for her."

Slocum chuckled.

"I saw the brothers you spoke about. They were drinking whiskey and talking to someone."

"They're looking for me."

"I thought about killing them, but I knew you could do it if you wanted to."

"No need to kill them for now. We better leave here at daybreak."

"I was thinking how big she was." Bear went off talking to himself. Slocum snuggled under the blankets and shut his weary eyes. He remembered the woman's great mounds of white flesh, and that made him want to find sleep faster.

14

The rain began to clear when they reached the badlands. Ragged clouds shredded the sky as they pushed eastward in the predawn. Water in the bottoms of the washes made the going slower. Out in the badlands, it appeared much less rain had fallen than in the Black Hills. Slocum twisted in the saddle, and could see Hainey's Peak shining in the shafts of sunlight.

Had the Great Spirit Woman of the Lakotas left their sacred hills? Snow Bear obviously felt so. Insulted and abandoned, she'd gone off somewhere else. Slocum remembered the Blackfeet ghost villages. Their god must have forsaken them too. That would be easy to believe. Kicking Dog had said the Great Spirit Woman would not answer him either when he sought her guidance.

Slocum and Snow Bear hurried onto the grasslands, and the wind found them. The sweeping force soon dried their clothes, and even Slocum's leather boots. Slocum knew it would be past dark before they found Kicking Dog's camp, but Snow Bear acted anxious to be home too. They topped a ridge, and Snow Bear stuck out his hand for Slocum to stop.

At the sight of the soldiers, they both turned their horses back and dropped under the rise. Slocum handed Snow Bear the reins to the dun and dug out his telescope. He dismounted, hoping they had not been seen by the soldiers or their scouts. His hat off, Slocum crawled on his belly to the crest.

He discovered in the telescope's eyepiece that the company of soldiers and two scouts had three white men lined up beside a wagon. A private in the wagon bed was holding up brown bottles to show the officer on horseback their stock in trade. Whiskey peddlers. The soldiers had caught them. Slocum eased back.

"Whiskey runners. I don't think the soldiers saw us. They were busy arresting them."

"Good, we will be more careful," Snow Bear promised, and handed him the dun's reins. Slocum mounted up and, taking their time, they swung north to avoid the patrol.

They reached the camp in the twilight. The dogs set up enough barking to bring everyone out of their tepees. Kicking Dog came out, looked at the blank face of Snow Bear, and nodded to acknowledge them, then shook his head. No need to tell the chief anything. He already knew by the look on Snow Bear's face that the medicine man had failed.

Slocum booted the dun off to White Swan's tepee. She rushed out to greet him, the long fringe whipping around her calves as she ran.

"How are things?" he asked, dismounting and preparing to undo the cinch.

She elbowed him aside to take charge of the unsaddling. "There is talk that they plan to ship us to the Indian Nation down in the south."

"Huh?" He searched around. "Who said such things?"

"It is a rumor." She shrugged, then looked at him with a troubled expression. "We have not left the reservation. We have not killed any white men or women. Why must we move?"

"They figure sooner or later that all your young men will join the wild ones unless they watch them closely."

"They may do that. They don't like this place on Wounded Knee Creek. They are mad. Maybe next, the white eyes will make us move to the White River Agency."

"I don't know what they will do."

She stripped the saddle and pads off the dun's wet back. Holding them in her arms, she nodded to him. "Turn him loose for me."

"Sure," he said as the daylight grew dimmer.

"I have some food hot for you." She led the way to the entrance of the tepee.

"Good, I'm near starved. Snow Bear and I have not eaten much real food in days."

"Did he find what he went for?"

"No," Slocum said softly.

"He didn't find the Spirit Woman?"

"He said she has fled."

"Where to?"

"I don't know." Slocum shook his head, standing up straight inside her tepee, the mild smoke of her fire teasing his nose. He was niggled by the notion of the two Abbott brothers being so close, but it still felt good to be back with her.

The camp was on the move the next morning, and Slocum pushed the dun horse along close to White Swan. She oversaw her four horses, and they dutifully trudged along. Children ran about with the camp dogs, playfully chasing them and expecting attention. Slocum felt at ease, despite knowing that the Abbott brothers were prowling the Black Hills looking for him. How they'd even had word he was headed this way, he had no way of knowing.

Perhaps their showing up at that remote mining camp was only blind luck. If they didn't talk to Greta or the stable man, they'd never know he'd passed through there. He doubted anyone else in Deadwood had had a good enough look at him to tell them much. The chances of their stumbling across Greta were slim. Besides, she didn't act like the mouthy kind. Still, he needed to move on. Word would be out soon enough that a white man was living with Kicking Dog's band.

"What do you think about?" White Swan asked, handing him the papoose board to hang on the saddle horn.

"Nothing," he lied to her. The notion of telling her that he would have to leave her soon made him feel uneasy. It would surely upset her, though he knew she expected him to ride on someday.

"What plans do you make?" she asked.

"I need to ride to Montana." He looked to the south and checked the sun. It was mid-morning. "I'm going the wrong way."

"If you go see this man, will you ride back by here?"

"You should not count on my return."

She nodded. "But if you can, will you come back to my lodge?"

"Yes, I will."

"Say no more. If you have places to go to, I will understand."

Slocum looked across the windswept short grass, and nodded. In the morning he would ride for Montana. He would thank Kicking Dog and Snow Bear and take his leave. The itching inside him to move on was bad enough. Leaving the Sioux was the only option for him to take.

When they stopped in mid-afternoon to camp for the night, Slocum could see up and down the draws. The bushes hung thick with crimson berries. It was a good place to lay over. He booted the dun toward where Kicking Dog sat his paint.

"Snow Bear says that you are anxious to see about Montana," the chief said.

"Snow Bear knows many things. When it will rain for days though there are no clouds. And when I have spoken to no one except her, he knows my plans."

"He feels you are his brother and these things that you ponder on, he knows."

"I will think further away." Slocum shook his head, taken aback by what the two men knew about him.

"Distance will be no barrier for him. Snow Bear will be with you, for you two are bonded."

"I am flattered."

"I wish that I knew more of your ways to deal with this agent. I see many things going wrong." Kicking Dog pursed his lips together in displeasure. "Then I know I must lead my people with or without my good friend. You said once it was easy to die. You were right."

"Have you seen Snow Bear?"

"He has gone off again to seek the Spirit Woman."

"He knew I planned to leave and did not wish to say good-bye?"

Kicking Dog agreed with a strong nod.

"Tell him I will think of him too."

"What was this mountain of a white woman he saw?" Kicking Dog asked, glancing around to be certain they were alone.

"The fattest, biggest whore I ever saw in my entire life."

"Hmm, he said so too." They both laughed.

15

Slocum rode out the next morning before White Swan even awoke. He quietly took his saddle and gear with him, caught the dun, and left the camp of the red berries. He short-loped the cow pony without daring to look back. He felt the gnawing at his gut, but he couldn't risk her life or anyone else's in a shoot-out with the Abbott brothers. It was simply better that he moved on.

He had to make sure he left no tracks for the Abbotts, avoiding any Indian camps and the army with their scouts, who were prowling the reservation for intruders, gunrunners, and buffalo hunters. He made good time, and felt by late afternoon he was close to reaching a portion of his goal, getting off the Rose Bud reservation. He kept the distant Black Hills to his left and traveled northwestward through the juniper-studded country.

At twilight, he ate some jerky from his saddlebags, watered the dun in a small stream, and threw down his bedroll. He hobbled the pony, then lay down and slept. Once during the night the nearby howling of wolves awoke him, but they moved away and he went back to sleep.

He caught the dun before dawn seamed the eastern horizon, and set out again. Near midday he spotted some wagons and signs of white people with them. So he reined the dun toward them. After weeks of mostly the Sioux language in his ears, the sound of English would be welcome.

"Howdy there, neighbor," the tall skinny man on the roan horse said, balancing a single-shot rifle over his lap. In his forties, the man wore brown britches patched repeatedly at both knees and a homespun blue shirt with deer-antler buttons. His galluses were of leather, black with sweat stains, and his beaver top hat looked like a dust pile. He spat tobacco to the side repeatedly to quiet the barking hounds and stock dogs with him.

"Howdy. You folks headed west?" Slocum asked

"We are, sir. And what be your destination?" He leaned aside and spat.

"Montana."

"Going there ourselves. Bufford Lane's my name. Got my wife, Mary, two strapping boys, and some more folks with young'uns here from Kentucky. The Blairs and the Dugans are the others. We all lived as neighbors back home."

"My name's Slocum. Mind if I join your group and ride along for a ways?"

"No, not at all, sir. We heard them Sioux was on the blood trail and I'd kind of be glad to have an ex'tree hand case they do attack."

"I think most of the hostile ones are west of the Black Hills, but you can't tell."

"Right. Mary, come over here," Lane shouted to the woman with the whip on her shoulder who was driving the oxen.

"Mary, this here is, Mr. Slocum," he said, and the young woman, in her late teens or early twenties, squinted her small red eyes at Slocum. He doubted she could see him.

"Nice to meet'cha," she said, and did a curtsy.

"Just Slocum's fine, ma'am," he said, and touched his hat brim. Lane's wife was obviously twenty years his junior. She turned to go back to driving her teams, and the supple shape of her youthful body was obvious under the wash-worn dress. There was something wrong with her eyes, he figured.

"Come on," said Lane. "You need to meet the Dugans. They have the next wagon."

Buster Dugan was a tall broad-shouldered man with a repeating rifle in his hand. He was afoot, and strode up and shook Slocum's hand. He had the wide-open face of a man who appraised you and after that was pleased to meet you. His flowing beard reached his chest, and his floppy-brimmed hat shaded his sharp eyes.

Mrs. Dugan looked uncomfortably pregnant as she sat on the wagon seat. She nodded cordially. Then Slocum and Lane rode back to the Blairs. Gary Blair was a short bulldog of a man with a spring in his walk as he drove his steers. His fat wife, Nan, came laughing from around the wagon, and Slocum was introduced. She was a happy-sounding woman with a brood of stair-step kids around her skirts. She had picked some wildflowers, and had a handful in her fist.

A couple of saddle ponies and three milk cows were being herded on foot behind the last wagon by Lane's two boys, Mark and Luther, in their teens. Barefoot and with britches too short, they nodded their freckled faces and grinned at their father's introduction of Slocum.

"You a buffalo hunter?" Mark asked.

"I have been."

"We thought we'd see lots of them shaggy creatures out here, but we ain't seen but maybe one or two and they run off."

"Most of them have been killed," Slocum said.

"I don't doubt that," Mark said, and shook his head.

"We could use one to eat," Lane said. "I'm tired of beans and corn bread."

"Maybe we can find one," Slocum said.

"Mister?" Mark called out.

Slocum reined his horse around to listen for the boy's question.

"Them Sioux as bad as they say they are out here?"

"The bad ones are."

Satisfied, the boy nodded glumly and switched with the willow limb at the lagging brindle cow.

"I don't want lots of talk about them savages upsetting the women. You understand?" Lane said under his breath.

"Sure. No need to do that."

"Thanks." Then Lane leaned over and spat.

In mid-afternoon they stopped at a stream for the oxen to graze. Slocum stayed back to watch the travelers unyoke the oxen and set up for the night. The three wagons were rolled up close enough to make them a fortress, putting everyone in the same proximity in case of an attack. Lane apparently knew a few things. As soon as the steers drank their fill of water, the two boys drove them to the nearby grass to feed.

"What would you do here?" Lane asked, squatting on his heels beside Slocum.

"Looks secure enough."

"I don't know much about Injuns, but I've listened good."

"You've done about all you can do with such a small group."

"Yeah, we never had money to go with them big trains. Man, it is a sight what they asked us to pay."

"You can be in Billings in a week."

"Much there?"

"Railroad town."

"Be kinda good to see folks again. You're the first face we've seen in a week. Guess we're off the main trail some, huh?"

"We should strike the railroad in another day or so."

"Good. You come eat with Mary and me. When she gets them fixed, we'll have plenty beans and corn bread."

"I've got some jerky—"

"No, you come eat. It'll be ready in an hour."

"Thanks. I may make a sweep and look for an antelope. Should be some up here."

"Fresh meat would sure be nice." Lane licked his tobacco-smeared lips.

Slocum tightened the cinch and swung back in the saddle. He jogged the dun from camp, feeling several eyes were on his back. He crossed the ridgeline and reined up. Nothing in sight. He moved across another wide basin, and then on high ground he spotted four yellow dots in the distance.

He reached into his saddlebags and drew out some white cloth. Then he reined the dun up to the tallest of the scattered junipers on the ridge. Standing in the stirrups, he tied the rag in the peak of the pungent-smelling evergreen. It unfurled like a flag, and he quickly rode out of sight with the rag snapping and popping in the strong wind.

The dun hobbled at the base of the hill, he took the Winchester and climbed back to lie on his belly and wait. Curiosity drew in antelopes. He hoped his plan worked. Fresh meat appealed more to him than either more jerky or beans.

In the short grass, he lay on his elbows, taking an occasional peek at the distant animals. A meadowlark sung close by, and some noisy ravens called out above the wind's rush. Slocum waited. Perhaps the antelopes couldn't see the streamer that waved above him and popped like a whip. He was about to give up when he saw one raise its goatlike head.

He held his breath. Maybe his plan would work. Then the small herd began to move toward him. He gave a grateful look at the clear sky, checked the breech, and satisfied the rifle was loaded, lay back down.

A half hour later, the curious antelope were coming in rifle range. Cautious at first, they sniffed the air and studied his flag. He needed them closer to make a clean shot. From under the boughs, he could see one of the does stamp her foot impatiently. He sized up a fat male and drew a bead on him, knowing one shot would be all he had time for. He held his breath and squeezed off a shot.

Blinded for an instant by the gunpowder smoke, he saw the buck go down, and waited to see if he rose up. The others were already out of rifle range, blurs racing away. Satisfied the animal was dead, he went to cut its throat to bleed it out. Then he hiked back after the dun. It was getting late, and the sun was fading. It took a tremendous effort for him to load the carcass over the saddle. He stepped up behind, gathered his rag from the bush on the way by, and headed for camp. They'd have meat to eat.

"Why, saints, Slocum has meat!" Lane shouted at his approach, and hushed the dogs.

"Kinda figured you was a hunter," Blair said, looking the buck over.

The men unloaded it, and they set up a tripod of poles to hang it on. All hands, with flashing knives, soon had the animal skinned, and Lane sent the boys after buckets of water while he carefully opened the body cavity. He handed out the liver and heart, then dropped the guts on the ground. His swift toe sent the first venturesome hound off yelping.

"Gawdamnit, I'll feed you when I get to it! Tie up these blasted dogs, someone!"

The dogs were gathered and tethered to wagon wheels and tongues. They whined and barked in anxious anticipation of the feast ahead. Lane drew out the kidneys and gave them to his wife. He washed out the cavity with buckets of water, and then turned to Slocum.

"How you want it cut up?"

"Best way to feed all of us."

A cheer went up as if they were surprised it was for all of them. Lane spat to the side and nodded. "I can do that. We'll slice some thin and cook it quick-like, and the rest we can roast. Boil the ribs all night and have them done for breakfast."

"Sounds like a good plan to me," Slocum said, and the others agreed.

"How did you ever get that close to one?" Mark asked.

"Tricked it. I'll show you how sometime."

"Boy, I'd sure like to learn how."

"Me too," Luther added.

The antelope feast lasted well into the night. The meat tasted good to Slocum, and he was full when he rose to his feet and bade the others, still feasting on bones, good night.

Over a chorus of thanks and waves from around the campfire, he took his bedroll and went out on the prairie. He studied the million stars, and stopped to gaze at the Bear Constellation. How was Snow Bear doing? Had the man ever reached the Great Spirit? He hoped so. Then he removed his gunbelt and boots, and lay down in his roll. For certain he would miss White Swan too. He closed his eyes to shut out the memory of her passionate times in bed with him.

He was up before dawn. He took a towel and headed for a quick dip in the stream before the others were awake. He was waist-deep in the water when someone came with a wooden pail. It was Mary Lane. She stopped at the water's edge and dipped her bucket in.

"I sure enjoyed that an-tee-lope that you shot last night," she said, straightening with her pail in both hands.

"It wasn't half bad," he said, grateful the water was up to his waist despite the darkness.

"That water cold to be a-bathing in?"

"Cold enough."

"It ain't Saturday yet, is it?"

"No, but I've missed a few Saturdays."

"Guess it won't hurt none then. What I mean is, it's okay for you to take an ex-tree one."

"I guess."

"I better get some coffee made. My old man wants his coffee ready when he gets up."

"Be a good idea then."

"Oh, yeah, he'll be up looking for it if I don't get back pretty soon. You take a bath often?"

"Whenever I can."

"Yeah." She swung the pail back and forth before her. "I better go. You come by and get some. I make strong coffee."

"I will, Mrs. Lane."

"Naw, Mary's good enough, Slocum."

"Yes, ma'am."

Could she see him, or had she guessed he was in the water? In the starlight, he could make her out, but as weak as her eyes looked to him, he doubted she saw him clearly. He shrugged the notion away and headed for shore before any of the others woke up and came down there.

He quickly dried off and dressed. Then he listened. He thought he heard a train whistle far off. They should start hearing more soon. The railroad couldn't be much further north.

16

"Smell that smoke?" Lane asked, riding beside Slocum.

"Been smelling it," Slocum said, surveying the rolling grassland without seeing any trace of a fire.

"Reckon that's Injuns?" Lane twisted around in the saddle with a grim look.

"We better ride ahead and go see."

"Be right back," Lane said to his wife, slicing the air with his rifle.

Both men spurred their horses into a lope, and soon reached the crest of a hill. The source of the smoke, they soon discovered, was a large camp of lodges. Buffalo hides were tossed over willow frames the way some of the Kansas Indians did. Slocum reined up the dun and Lane put his roan in beside him. There were wagons parked around, some with canvas covers and others with bows that stood out like the ribs on a dead cow.

"Injuns?" Lane asked.

"I think it's a camp of breeds. I heard they were up here," Slocum said, recalling the stories he'd heard about the outcasts banding together in dangerous gangs.

"Breeds?" Lane frowned. "They dangerous?"

"They'll do to watch. They ain't white and they aren't red, so they have no reservation."

"We going down there?"

"We better. Them dogs are yapping and they've seen us."

"Yeah, I'd rather meet them than run off like a damn cur dog and have them come seeking me."

"Exactly."

A few squaws looked hard at the two men and drove the barking dogs back with switches. A tall sultry-looking woman in her twenties came out of a lodge, her silver jewelry glinting brightly in the sun. Her reddish dark hair hung in long braids, wrapped in ermine fur. She said something to someone in the lodge, and a man appeared. His hair was snow-white on the right and black as coal on the left. He was bare-chested, with a great medal hanging on a ribbon from his neck.

Other men began to emerge from their lodges and drift toward this man, who was obviously the leader. They had wary gazes and their looks of suspicion ran deep.

"Ho." The man made a peace sign and Slocum returned it.

"We're going west and smelled the smoke of your fires," Slocum said.

"You have a good horse. Would you sell him?" the man asked.

"No, I need him to ride on. My name is Slocum and this is Lane."

"I am Bobby Devereau."

"Nice to meet you."

"You hide hunters?"

"No. Mr. Lane is a farmer. I am a cattle driver."

"You have many cattle?" His interest came alive.

"In Texas." Slocum considered that a good enough answer.

"You must pay a toll fee to pass here."

"What the hell—" Lane blurted out before Slocum could stop him.

"How much is that?" Slocum asked.

"Ten dollars a wagon."

"Why, that's—" Lane said with his face reddening with anger.

Slocum frowned and shook his head to silence the man. No need to rile up this camp of husky bucks. There were over a dozen of them that he could count. He and Lane needed to bargain a little or dicker on the price first. Then, if it was still too high, they could get tough, but two against that many were poor odds.

"We don't have much," Slocum said.

"Then you must go around our land," Devereau said.

"He got a deed to this damn country?" Lane asked behind his hand.

"No, but he's got the will to charge us."

"I ain't paying him shit," Lane whispered.

"Settle down, we ain't through dealing with them." Slocum was about to lose his patience with Lane.

"I guess we'll have to talk to the others about the toll," Slocum said to Devereau. "We can't pay for all of them." He hoped his bluff about "all of them" would work.

"We will come by to collect," Devereau said.

"In that case, we'll see you," Slocum said, and reined his horse around, but not before he looked the chief's woman over good. She wasn't half bad-looking. Lane followed him, and Slocum had an itchy feeling on the back of his neck until they crossed over the ridge.

"What're we going to do about them?" Lane asked.

"Load every damn gun in camp and hope to hell we can hold them off."

"They coming after us?"

"Those kind prey on the small wagon trains. The ones like yours with only a few guns."

"But what if we pay them the toll?"

"I don't figure it would make a damn bit of difference. We are going to be vulnerable until we reach civilization. How much ammo you got?"

"Maybe a couple hundred rounds, rifles, shotguns, pistols, and all."

"Then we can't waste a shot."

"The army out here?"

"You seen them since you started across here?"

"No."

"That answers your question. From now on everyone is armed at all times. No one strays from the camp. Graze the steers close by and under guard." Slocum mentally went over what else they could do.

"I wish to hell we hadn't gone over there," Lane said.

Slocum reined up the dun and looked at the three wagons toiling westward. "Wouldn't have made any difference. He or one of his men would have spotted you sooner or later."

Lane took off his top hat and scratched his uncombed thatch of graying dark hair. "I may wish I'd never left Kentucky."

"No, we've got to make them breeds believe that they've found a hornet's nest."

"Damn, Slocum, you can ride on. They'd never catch you."

He shook his head slowly. "Lane, I won't ride out on you or your people."

"You're a damn fool not to."

"I've been called worse. Let's have a meeting. We need to be ready for anything."

They booted their horses for the train.

"Them breeds want how much toll fee?" Blair asked as they sat on the ground in a circle: the three wives, the two boys, the three men, and the four small children who played unmoved by the news that paled the others. Slocum considered the breeds trouble with a capital T.

Lane held up his hand. "They want ten bucks a wagon to let us pass, but Slocum says it won't make a damn if we pay them or not."

"Let's pay them and see first," Mrs. Dugan said.

"No, they will take your money and still try to rob you of all you have." Slocum shook his head. "They don't think like you do. They would collect and then still go after you. I'm sorry, but their ways aren't like white people."

"What can we do then?" the pregnant woman asked.

"Be armed and prepared to defend this train."

"I'll take my husband's shotgun and use it," she announced.

"Don't waste any shells," Slocum said.

"Slocum, if I shoot it, there will one less breed in this world."

"Yes, ma'am."

"I'll get one with it or not shoot it."

"Good enough," Slocum said, not doubting the woman's sincerity. "You boys can take turns riding ahead as advance scouts, but only a short distance from the train. Like on the rises, so we have warning if they're coming and can gather up."

"What will we do at night?" Lane asked.

"Stake some of these hounds at a distance from the camp as sentinels."

"Won't the breeds kill them?" Dugan asked.

"Perhaps, but we may have time to defend ourselves," Lane said.

Slocum agreed.

"When do you think they'll try us?"

"Soon. We push hard, we should reach the railroad in a few days. We can find a telegraph there and wire for the army. Those breeds'll know once we strike north what our plans are."

"Will there be a telegraph?"

"There's one along the railroad."

"Good," Lane said. "Daylight's burning. Let's head north."

Satisfied with the plan, Slocum made sure each of the boys carried a cap-and-ball pistol. Mrs. Blair had a Long Tom shotgun in the wagon box beside her seat. Mary Lane had a small-caliber rifle in the crook of her arm. Slocum guessed a .22. Mrs. Dugan carried a single-shot, lever-action rifle. Armed and ready, they swung the lead teams in a northward direction, and the rest followed.

Slocum hoped the whistle he had heard was a train. He rode ahead, sending Mark to stay on the left flank, feeling that that was the direction the breeds would come from.

By late afternoon they reached a shallow river. The oxen grew weary, and he knew if they grew too tired they would lie down. You couldn't drive an old steer to his death. They'd quit first.

After several passes back and forth on the dun, he felt the ford would be easy. Lane sat his horse on the bank and agreed with his assessment.

"Let's double-team the crossing," Slocum said. "Then they won't have to pull so hard."

"Good idea. Mary, get in the wagon," Lane said.

"No, I drive them steers. I'll drive them across."

"Did you hear me?"

"I'm going to drive them across," she said, and cracked the whip. "They can pull it."

Lane reined the horse around and frowned at her belligerence. The first span never hesitated, and with Mary talking to them, both spans of oxen soon were wading into the water. She raised the hem of her dress and went with them. It soon became impossible for her to hold the hem, and she fought the current with her hand on the last steer for support.

Her voice commands and coaxing soon had the short-legged steers belly-deep in the river. With effort she made difficult steps beside them, her skirt a hindrance. The teams stopped, and she managed to snap the whip over them.

Slocum feared she would be swept away at any moment. With a hand on the yoke, she began to shout at them. "Damn, you devils, get out of here!"

At her abrupt command, they pressed into the yokes and the wagon began to move again. The travelers on the south bank looked on and held their breath. Slocum sat the dun, ready to bail into the stream and either save her or force the steers to go on.

The wagon's canvas top lurched from side to side as it began to move over the rocks. Soon, to Slocum's relief, the lead team began to climb the bank. Mary held up her saturated dress as she fought her way up beside them.

A cheer went up, and Blair started his team across.

"Don't worry, Slocum, we're going to do it too!" the pregnant woman shouted at him. She held on to the spring seat as the wagon teetered from side to side going into the water.

Slocum waited on the shore until Blair and his wagon were across, followed by the Dugans and the loose stock. When they were all on the other side, he signaled for Mark to come in from his post on the ridge. Then the two of them forded the river.

"No sign of the breeds," the boy said, riding beside him.

"Don't think they aren't out there. They are and they're waiting for their time."

"Yes, sir."

On the north beach, Slocum took a last long look at the sweeping grassland dotted with some dark junipers on the ridges. He would feel a lot better when they reached the railroad. It couldn't be much further—a day or two at the most, by his guess.

17

Slocum jerked awake in the darkness. He was sleeping sitting up with his back to the wagon wheel. A hound tied down at the river was barking hard. Slocum lurched to his feet, rifle in his hands, and rushed to try to see across the silver ribbon of water in the dim light.

"There's one of them!" Dugan shouted from beside him, and let loose with a fiery red charge from his shotgun.

The result was the scream of a horse blasted by the pellets, then bucking off with several more horses following. Their hooves clattered off in the night, and soon only the hush of the river could be heard.

"I got 'em," Dugan said.

"You scared hell out of them anyway," Lane said, standing in his underwear beside them, armed with his rifle. "You think they're gone for the night?" he asked Slocum.

"I don't take anything for granted."

"Damn good idea. Go back to bed, everyone, but them on guard stay there. They could come back," Lane said, and gave a big yawn. "Sons-a-bitches. It's going to be hell, ain't it, Slocum?"

"Looks that way."

"I figure they have to stop us now, 'cause we know who they are."

"Yes, you have a real point." Slocum looked off toward

the dark horizon. They had some real adversaries out there, who damn sure wouldn't give up easily.

They broke camp at sunup without making a fire. Slocum worried about the Blair children. They looked haggard and worried. He watched their smiling mother load them in the wagon and give him a firm nod.

"Be better in there, won't they?" she asked him politely.

"Yes, ma'am."

"And Mr. Slocum, I sure want to thank you. Our men are fighters, but they ain't use to this kinda warfare. You're a blessing, sir, to stay with us."

"It'll work out all right," he said to dispel her doubts.

"If it does, it will because of the likes of you, sir."

"Thanks," he said, and rode the dun around to where Mark sat a small bay horse bareback.

"Same plan as yesterday? I'll stay on the ridge and keep riding along with the train?" the youth asked.

"See anything, you burn a path back here. Wait. Is one of these hounds yours?"

"Yes sir, that redbone."

"Take him along. They have a good nose and may smell trouble before you see it."

"Sure. Come on, Rowdy," he called to the dog, who beat his tail on the grass, obviously flattered to be invited along.

"I'll ride out front?" Lane asked Slocum. "Man, you were right. They came at night and we could have all been scalped."

"We may have taught them a lesson. I was upset at first that Dugan shot, but it turned out well and the shot was not wasted."

"I did some soldiering, Slocum, and I've seen officers before. You must have been a helluva commander."

"Just ordinary, did what I had to do."

"You can tell me that, but I don't need to believe it." Lane slapped his roan on the butt to turn him. "Maybe we'll find the railroad today."

"I hope so."

The wagons rolled until mid-morning, then made a stop. Slocum saw Mark waving, and rode out to talk to him.

"I seen some sign of them trailing us." Mark pointed to the south. "They're keeping back and I only catch glimpses of them."

"How many did you see?"

"Oh, four or five. How many are there?"

"I guessed a dozen. They must have divided up."

"Where's the others at?" the boy asked.

"Good question. Don't let them cut you off from the wagons. Ride back to the train whenever you think you need to. Don't take any chances. We'll need everyone if they attack."

"I'll keep an eye out."

"Good," Slocum said, and loped back to camp.

Lane came riding in on the roan and pulled up before him. "This depression we're in gets narrower up ahead. They'd have cover in the cedars on both sides of the slopes and be close enough to take shots at us."

"Good thinking. Why don't you ride up on the ridge and see if we can go down it."

"Sure thing. Mark see them?"

"Yes, he seen part of them and they've split up, so be careful up there."

"Damn. I'm going up there now." Lane rushed off on his roan.

"Ain't any place to run a wagon up there," Dugan said to Slocum, motioning to the ridge.

"It won't be easy going, I know, but we don't need to ride into a trap either. Lane says it's too narrow up ahead."

He could see Mrs. Blair holding a crying child and rocking it. They had plenty of reason to be upset. He wished he could do more for their safety.

Lane came boiling back. "Rocky up there, be hell to try and take the wagons that way."

"What about the far side? Is it wider between the ridges."

"No," Lane said. "This country all narrows. Ridges get taller and the valleys narrower."

The breeds probably knew that too. Slocum wondered how he would ever be able to get the train by the breeds if their plan was to ambush the train.

"I want everyone to stay in camp. Let the oxen graze. We won't move out until dark."

"How we going by them then?" Lane looked worried.

"We stay close together, have the dogs as sentries, and use our heads, we may survive a charge through them."

"They'll swarm us."

"They know we have shotguns. I think if they are used right, we can put enough fear in them to back off. Their rifles won't be as good in the dark if they can't see what they're shooting at."

"They won't stop till we're dead or they're defeated, will they," Lane said, looking off at the far ridge.

"That's the way I figure it."

"Lord, why did I ever leave Kentucky?"

"To settle a new land. We're headed there."

Lane let out a sigh. "I'll go tell the others we're staying here awhile."

Slocum waved Mark in from the ridge. The youth came riding back, dropped off the bareback horse, and drew himself a gourd of water from the barrel on the side of the wagon.

"What next?" he asked.

"Those hounds hunt coons?" Slocum asked him.

"They sure do, but I ain't seen one out here since way back in Minnesota. Don't think they got any out here."

"If we had some scent, would they track it?"

"I got some coon scent in some pill bottles. You need it?"

"We will in a little while."

"What are you going to do with it?"

"You'll see. Let that pony of yours graze some."

"I swear, Slocum, what are you up to?" Lane asked, looking mildly amused.

"My plan is to leave a scent trail through them cedars up ahead that those hounds will take up and go a-bawling. They start in there, how will those breeds know they aren't after them? They don't know anything about treeing dogs, and the dogs sound ferocious."

"It might work."

"It's going to work. Have everyone tie up their hounds. Get some sacks and we'll douse them with Mark's scent and ride like hell through those cedars dragging that smell before those breeds get set up in them."

"What if they figure it out?" Lane asked.

"How're they going to do that?"

"Blamed if I know, and it's a better plan than I could think up."

Lane, on his roan, carried one sack on a rope. Slocum carried the other, and they rode out of camp with the two small bottles in his vest pocket.

"Keep your hand on that rifle. We may find them up there in that brush," Slocum warned Lane, and booted the dun in close. He doused the scent on Lane's sack and then on his own.

The man pulled down the narrow brim on his top hat and nodded. "Let's go."

They were off. The rope tied to his horn, the Colt in his right hand, Slocum sent the dun charging through the junipers on the west slope. The dragging sack sometimes became hung up, and the rope grew tight over his leg in places, but the sack soon pulled loose and came flying after his horse. On the other side of the draw, on the slope over there, he could see Lane pressing his roan through the boughs on the fly.

At last Slocum could see the open expanse of prairie. He sent the dun downhill and tossed the sack in the top of a tall evergreen. Lane did the same thing on his side, and then rode over to join him.

Slocum looked in time to spot a rider on the west ridge turn his pony away and disappear. Good, they would be curious now that they'd had an observer who'd seen them. If the breeds were even half as superstitious as most Indians, they would be upset. More so when they found the sacks in the trees with no indication what they meant. It was the only plan he had and it needed to work. There were innocent lives at stake.

The quarter moon began to rise when Slocum left Lane to lead the way. The Lane and Dugan wagons were side by side. The Blair wagon was behind. Slocum rode around to talk to the boys. Mark and Luther were in the rear of the group with plenty of firepower. Besides three fully loaded cap-and-ball pistols, they each had a shotgun.

"You boys fire at anything out there that moves or shoots at us."

"We will, Slocum," Mark said.

"But don't do it until you see something certain. We aren't that overcome with ammunition."

"We can do it."

"I know that," Slocum said, and wheeled the dun around to join Lane. Besides his .44 Colt, he had his boot gun, the .30.

"You figure they're up there?" Lane asked.

"Yes, and we get closer, you and I are siccing those hounds on them."

"Sure hope it works." Lane twisted in the saddle, obviously checking on his wife, who was driving their wagon.

"It will."

The wagons creaked along in the darkness. Slocum wet his lips as he rode, trying to keep everything in prospective. A little closer, they'd let the hounds loose. The dogs were hard to keep quiet, and they occasionally bawled as if they had scented the track. Slocum could make out the dark shadows of the thickest brush ahead.

He nodded to Lane, and they rode to the rear of his wagon. They tied their horses to the tailgate, and the Blair children began to pass out hounds to them. Lane held them on leashes as the kids made a game of dragging the hounds to the tailgate, then two of them helping to give each hound over to Slocum.

Soon the seven hounds were on the ground. When the children whispered that that was all of them, Slocum thanked them. It was a job to contain the hounds. They leaped and whined in excitement, knowing something was about to happen.

Lane sorted the hounds as they tugged hard on the restraints. He gave Slocum three of them. As Slocum started out with the pack, they were so eager they pulled him along. Lane went to the far side with his whining and plunging wards.

"Now!" Slocum shouted, satisfied Lane was in place. The night filled with the hounds' mournful barks. Slocum ran for his horse, and collided with Lane mounting his roan.

"The trap's set," Slocum shouted, and hurried the dun to the front, his Colt in his fist. On the hillsides the mournful cries of the hounds filled the air. The men and Mary pushed the oxen with their whips and voices. Slocum and Lane rushed forward, filling the sky with gunshots.

It wasn't a stampede in the night, but the steers were moving faster than he had ever seen them. The charging, barking dogs were drawing some guttural shouts. Slocum reloaded the Colt while riding on his head-bobbing dun.

"They out there?" Lane asked, pulling in close to him while they waited for the wagons to catch up.

"Yes. I heard one of them scream."

Then the boys at the back opened fire, and Slocum raced back to help them. He could see several of the breeds on horseback beating a path over the west ridge. He reached the rear, and saw a few attackers in the wagon tracks taking potshots at the train.

Luke and Mark's shotgun blasts silenced them.

"Good shooting." Slocum reined the dun around and searched the slopes for any sign. The wagons rumbled along.

"Slocum!" Lane shouted, and collided his roan into the dun. "They've got Mary."

"Which way?"

"West. I was afraid to shoot."

"That was best. Stay with the train and get them through. Camp at the next water north. I'll get her back and join you as soon as I can."

"I want to go along."

"No, we both can't leave. You need to take care of this train. I'll get your wife back."

"God be with you, man."

Slocum would need God and all the other help he could get. With no time for more words, he sent the dun westward and up the slope through junipers. He topped out and reined the pony in. Nothing in sight. He had to trust his own judgment that the breeds would go back to their camp with Mary.

He dropped off the ridge and headed in that direction. He had to get after them fast for Mary's safety. He didn't like the prospects of what they might do to her. On the level ground, he sent the dun into a hard run.

Racing this hard across the prairie in the moonlight was dangerous. Badger and prairie-dog holes were everywhere, and one misstep would cost him the dun. But with the wind in his face, he threw caution to the wind and hurried the pony on.

18

The dun was about to give out. From his place, Slocum could see the dark shapes of the breeds' lodges in the starlight. He hoped his arrival was a surprise and they weren't expecting him. Short of their camp, he reined up, stepped off, jerked the Winchester out of the boot, and left the heaving pony standing there. He'd tend to him later. Slocum hurried toward the wagons.

He used the first vehicle for cover. With the rifle in his hands, he searched around in the silver light for any movements or sounds. Plenty of snorting, tired horses were about the camp. From what he observed, the lodges were dark. Most of the breeds must have already gone to sleep.

"Don't move a muscle." The barrel of a pistol was pressed hard in Slocum's back. One thing flashed through his mind. How had he made such a stupid mistake?

Slocum raised his hands, and felt the man remove his Colt and large knife from the sheath. He still had the pistol in his boot. Maybe, just maybe, they wouldn't find it. Still, Slocum would have to raise his pants leg to get at it, which could get himself shot in the process.

"I have him," the man shouted out.

"Good, bring him over here." Slocum knew that was Devereau's voice.

"Well, big man, where are your damn dogs at now?" Devereau said when Slocum finally stood before him.

"They'll be here to eat your ass off before long," Slocum replied. He could make out the leader with his half-white head of hair in the dim light, along with several of the others.

"Ha. Now you are not there to lead them. Good, I will kill them slowly and rape their women while they watch and die."

"Don't count on it. They'll plant your heads on sticks if you even try."

"You talk plenty tough for a man about to die."

"Not me, friend. You are the one set to die."

"No, big man, those stupid farmers won't know what to do without you to sic those damned dogs on us."

"They weren't my dogs."

"Tie him up and put him in the lodge with the woman. I want him to die very slow. We will ride at dawn and kill all of them with the wagons. After that we will come back and have a feast and torture him to death. Slow-like." In the starlight Slocum could see the man's wicked grin.

Two of them shoved Slocum toward a dark lodge, and once he was inside, thrust tight his arms and legs with rawhide strips. When the second man stood up, he kicked Slocum hard in the side of the gut.

"There, you sumbitch!" With that, he went out of the lodge after the other.

Slocum could not move. His breath came in ragged gasps. But he still had the gun in his boot. All he needed to do was get loose. He strained at his bindings, but they did not give.

"Slocum?"

It was Mary Lane calling to him in a soft voice. He stopped struggling and answered her. "Yes."

"How can we get away from them?" she asked in the voice of a scared child.

"Are you bound up tight?" He tried to see her, but in the dark lodge, he made out nothing.

"Yes, my arms are."

"Get over here. There's a knife in my boot. Maybe you can get it out."

"Where are you?"

"Come to my voice—no, I hear someone coming. Stay there."

The sound of rawhide soles on the ground stopped at the door, and someone threw back the flap. Belly-down on the buffalo robe, Slocum turned his head to try and see who it was.

Soon the intruder lighted a candle in a holder. It was the tall woman. The red-orange flames reflected from her face. She went to where Mary sat on a crate and put the candle down.

"So he stole you, huh?" she demanded, then reached out and with both hands ripped Mary's dress open to the waist.

Mary gave a sharp gasp.

Slocum strained at his bounds. What was she up to? He watched her cup Mary's left breast in her hand. She ran her long brown fingers around the globe, and a small smile crept into her face.

"You have sorry tits. I will show you real ones." Quickly she stripped off the fringed deerskin blouse, then stuck out her long breasts in Mary's face.

"See, here are real ones. Mine are longer and much firmer than yours. Why would Bobby want to play with yours?" Then she laughed again. An evil contemptuous laugh that was intended to taunt, not bring humor.

"Stand up!" she ordered.

"W-why?" Mary stammered.

"I said stand up. When Felicia speaks, you obey her. Stand up!"

"What for?" Mary asked, sounding bewildered.

In a rage, Felicia jerked her up, then tore the dress completely open. Mary tried to turn away, but Felicia forced her to look at her. Then Felicia shoved Mary's underwear down and stepped back to look.

"You ever had a baby?"

"No."

"Maybe he wants you to have babies for him. You're ugly. I don't know why he brought you here." She lifted the lamp as if to look closer at her.

Slocum found no slack in his bindings. What was the

woman up to? Obviously, she was jealous of the fact that her man had brought Mary there.

"He should have raped and killed you. Spread your legs apart." Felicia advanced on her.

"No, I won't—" The resounding slap of Felicia's hand to Mary's face made Slocum cringe. He watched the woman step in close and grab for Mary's pubic area.

Mary gave a cry. Felicia's face showed signs of pleasure as she probed the girl.

"Oh, you say. My, my, do you like that?" Felicia asked.

"No."

"You will like it better when he fills it."

"No."

"Yes, you will. It will be better than dying." She continued to probe Mary with her finger. "Yes, you will forget your old ways. You will be the second wife of the chief. And you will be my slave too. Doesn't my finger feel good in there?"

"No."

"It will," Felicia said, and removed her finger to wipe it on Mary's open dress. "I will teach you things to like."

Then she turned and glanced down at Slocum. "A shame I have no time for you. You might be very interesting. Maybe I will look to see how big you are."

At the sound of voices outside, she turned her head and made a displeased face. "I better go see what he wants. I'll look at you later," she said, speaking directly to him.

Slocum hoped not. He could hear Mary sobbing. The woman blew out her candle and left the lodge.

Slocum listened to be certain she was gone. Damn, what a mess. "Mary," he hissed. "Get over here."

"I can't, I'm naked," she cried.

"Gawdamnit, get over here. We've got to get the hell out of here and fast."

"But how?" she moaned, coming across the room. "Don't look at me."

"I can't see a damn thing in here without the light. Get down and find that knife in my boot. We've got to hurry."

Her shoes found him. "Wait. I have to get my underwear off. It has my feet tied."

She sat down in the dark and kicked to get rid of her underwear.

"There," she finally said, and moved around on her butt, feeling with her hands bound behind her back. "Which boot?"

"The right one. Quick, go back, someone's coming," he hissed at the sound of footsteps.

"Oh, not her again," Mary moaned.

"Go, before they come in and get suspicious," he said under his breath.

"Oh, dear God—" She struggled to get up, and was back on the crate when the flap swung back for Devereau's entry.

Devereau lighted a match and held it up. Mary twisted and turned away, holding her head aside.

"Has someone come to examine the merchandise?" he asked, then kicked Slocum in the leg. The match went out and darkness filled the lodge. The sharp pain in Slocum's leg made cold chills run down the side of his neck.

"Who tore her dress off?"

"Ask you wife," Slocum managed.

Devereau laughed in the darkness and moved to Mary. "Did she want to see your titties? Ah, they are smaller than hers." Mary was fussing and trying to escape, but Slocum knew the breed was mauling and fondling her all over.

"Ah, you will be fun when I return. Maybe I should give you some now."

"Bobby, let's ride!" someone outside shouted.

"No time for you now, little mink. I will give you plenty later. All right, I'm coming!" He stomped outside, cussing under his breath.

The sounds of their horses drummed off into the night, and Slocum could hear Mary sobbing. He had no time for sympathy. He needed to get free and go help the others.

"Mary, get over here. We need that knife now."

"Oh, what will I do?"

"Get the knife and be quick about it so we can escape."

He heard her shuffle over as she sobbed. At last, with her back to him, she fumbled to pull up his pants leg. He could feel her small fingers bound together moving down his leg.

Could she reach deep enough?

"It's no use," she wailed.

"I agree," he said in defeat. "You scoot up here and I'll try to chew off your bindings."

"Will that work?" she asked, bumping around beside him.

"Damned if I know, but something has to."

When she was in place, he tried to fasten his teeth on the leather straps at her wrist. He could only get a small bite. His neck soon cramped and he was forced to stop.

"What's wrong?" she asked.

"It's awkward. I'll be fine in a minute." He went back and bit on the leather some more. It was strong, and his front teeth soon began to ache, but a small slit had been opened and the wet leather was stretching.

But with no hands to help him, Slocum knew it would be a long job. She patiently held her hands toward him.

"I'm worried about the people at the train," she said absently.

"They can hold out if they do it right." He gnawed more on the leather, but his progress proved exceedingly slow. If he couldn't work faster, his teeth would give out first.

"It's getting looser," she said.

"Good," he replied, wanting to hook his eyetooth over it and grind away. If only his teeth were sharper.

"Quick, someone's coming," he hissed at the sound of footfalls.

"Oh, no," Mary groaned, and finally managed to get to her feet. Seated on her crate again, she turned her head away.

The person went by and did not come inside. Slocum listened, and then hissed for her to come back. He tried to chew and rip. The rawhide was not giving that he could tell. He would have to rest and then go back and fight it.

Daylight began to filter in from the smoke hole and around the flap. The tear in the leather wasn't half an inch larger. He could see the wet rawhide when he paused to rest. Her hands were looser. Of course, he realized, the rawhide would stretch when wet. He began to bring up more saliva and worked on chewing it.

"Try to get loose," he finally said, out of breath.

"There!" she said, and shucked her bindings. She clutched the dress shut with both hands.

"Forget it, I'm not looking at you. Get my knife and cut me loose."

"I will," she said, and soon had the jackknife from his boot. She began to saw his feet ties first, and he finally felt them loosen. He managed to sit up, and she moved behind him, holding the dress closed with one hand and the knife in the other.

"Good girl," he said, at last free and rubbing his sore wrists to get the circulation in his hands started. Then came the pins and needles, and he knew the circulation was returning.

"Oh, what will I do?" she asked, holding the dress together.

"Look around, there may be some clothes in here." He reached down in his boot and drew out the small handgun. A flood of relief went through him. They were free at last and had a loaded gun.

"There are some man's clothing is all," she complained, displeased at the filthy items she found.

"Put them on," he said, moving to the flap to look to see what he could.

"They're pants."

"Mary, put them on or wear that torn dress. We have to get out of here."

She made a sound of revulsion. He glanced over to see her poke a bare shapely calf in one leg. When he peeked out of the lodge, he couldn't see anything or anyone moving outside, but that didn't mean they had all gone. Felicia, he felt, could be a warrior too if she wished. He turned back. Mary had stripped off the dress, and was putting on a faded blue military blouse.

"They stink," she said. "I may get fleas from them."

"Better fleas than a grave or a breed husband. You about ready?"

"What will we do out there if there are very many of them?" She completed buttoning the too-large shirt.

"Shoot as many as we have to. Now come on and stay close to me."

"Slocum—"

"Come on," he insisted with impatience. In a quick sweep, he recovered his hat from the floor and put it on.

She wound up the long sleeves, then nodded that she was ready. He moved the flap aside enough and slipped outside. The bright light of the first rays of the sun blinded him for a second. He searched quickly around when his vision cleared, holding the Colt ready in his fist. Seeing nothing, he told her to come out.

Then he remembered her bad eyes when she felt blindly for him.

"I can't see."

"I know," he said. "Take my hand and move with me."

"I'll try," she said, and came along.

She really could not see, he quickly realized. "Can you see with a sunbonnet on?"

"Only shapes and outlines. But in this bright sun I can't see a thing."

"Never mind, stay close."

"I will," she promised, and he herded her in the direction of his dun horse, which he had spotted standing ground-tied.

A squaw began shouting, "They are getting away!"

Slocum turned and raised the Colt up to eye level. A breed with a rifle rushed out of a lodge, and only had time to straighten before the .30 spoke and sent him flying backward. Struck in the face, he would be no problem. As a shield for Mary, Slocum backed toward the dun. Gun ready, he watched the lodges for any other breeds, but none of them ventured outside.

"Get in the saddle," he said to her, and saw her climb up.

Felicia came out and shouted at him. "Bobby will get you! He'll make you and that white bitch pay."

Apparently she was unarmed. Slocum didn't take her threat that seriously. Devereau had to catch them first, and Slocum didn't intend to let that happen. He swung up behind Mary, and had to agree the clothing she wore did smell bad.

"Let's get out of here," he said, and she reined the dun around under his guidance.

He booted the dun into a long trot, looking back to see if there was any threat rushing out of those lodges. He only saw women and children gathering around the dead man.

"What if we meet them?" she asked.

"Let's hope we don't." He studied her weak eyes, then stuck his hat on her head. "There that might help some."

"Thank you," she said, turning in the saddle.

Once they were over the crest, he decided they had no pursuit and needed to slow down to save the poor dun. He reined him up, and they took a leisurely pace down the wide rolling grassland.

"You been married long?" he asked.

"Six months. Lane's wife died and he asked for my hand. I thought it was too soon and me being near blind, well, I never expected anyone to want me. Figured I'd be an old maid. I was twenty when we wed. Most girls in Kentucky have five kids by that time."

"Guess you'll have kids someday of your own."

She shrugged her shoulders under the too-large blouse. "He's had two wives and those boys was by the first one. She never had no more, and the second one, Ida, she never had any. I knew Ida, and she was a healthy girl when they got married. They never had none in five years. He kinda warned me we might never have one."

"How did Ida die?"

"Scarlet fever. Took a lot of folks in our community last winter. She got it bad. I went over to help her and she died that very night. We buried her the next day and Lane, he said I should marry him and go west with him."

"You agreed?"

"Not at first. I thought it was too soon. But he said life was for the living and you just better live it for the day. Tomorrow, he said, you could be like poor Ida, dead."

Slocum looked back, saw nothing. It was time to make the dun trot again or they'd never never catch the others. Slocum booted him to go faster. He wondered how the wagon people were holding out. If they'd made a good defensive stop, they should be all right. They had the ammunition to hold off the breeds if they used it wisely.

He would feel a lot better when the two of them caught up with the others. In the distance a raven screamed, and he twisted to look over his shoulder. A chill ran up his spine, but he saw nothing. He turned back to the rhythmic roll of the dun's gait, and could still smell the sweat and horse odors on the dirty blouse Mary wore.

She had to reach up with one hand to hold on to his hat. He wanted to grin. The size was way too large for her, but he hoped it gave her eyes some relief. Her tangled short brown hair bounced with the horse's stride. They had miles to go.

Hours later, Slocum heard the scattered shots ahead. Mary twisted in the saddle and with a look of fear asked, "Are they still alive?"

"I hope so, Mary. Someone's still shooting."

"What will we do?"

"First, we must find the breeds' horses and we will steal them."

"Steal them?"

"Yes. On foot the breeds won't be near as dangerous."

"Where will the horses be?"

"I figure some boy is watching them over the hill from the shooting."

"But where?"

He reached past her, took the reins, and sent the dun for the ridge. "We have to find them."

From the high point, he could see the canvas tops of the three wagons parked close together in the distance on a large stretch of prairie. The breeds were obviously bellied down around them and taking potshots. From the sounds of things, the wagon folks were either spacing their shots or out of ammo. He hoped they were doing as he'd told them to do.

"I can hear the horses, they must be over there," she said, pointing down the draw.

"Good," he said, and slipped off the dun's rump. Somewhere down there they'd probably left a boy to herd them. He had to locate him and disarm him first, then take the horses.

"What are we going to do?"

"You're going to stay here."

"No, don't leave me alone, please?" she pleaded, about to cry.

"You can come a little ways, but be quiet." He took her hand.

He caught the dun's rein and started down the slope. He didn't need a blind woman to care for, but she was his responsibility. He kept to the junipers for cover, hoping that the herder was sleeping on the job or not paying much attention, thinking the danger was over the hill.

More distant rifle shots. Slocum fretted about Mary's safety if they did meet a breed. Keeping her behind him, he searched for signs of the horse herd.

"You hear that music?" she asked in a hushed voice.

"No, all I hear is wind." He craned his head around to try to find the herd, holding the dun up close by the reins.

"I hear it. It is a flute." She cupped her hand to her ear.

"What is it playing?"

" 'Gary Owen,' I think." She gripped the stirrup for a guide. "It is ahead of us somewhere."

Damn, who was playing a flute? He still could not hear it. Then the wind stopped and he too heard the notes. It wasn't a military flute player making the music. Probably one of the breed boys.

"Stay here," he said, and handed her the reins. She nodded her head under the too-big hat, and he hurried off, carefully using the junipers for cover.

He soon located the flute player. A young boy so intent on his instrument, he never heard Slocum sneak up behind him. When Slocum pressed the small Colt's muzzle to his temple, the boy's face blanched near white.

"On your belly," Slocum ordered, and quickly trussed tight the boy's hands and feet. Gagged and bound, the boy moaned, and Slocum straightened.

"Consider it lucky you are alive," he said, and hurried back to find Mary.

"I'll go catch their horses and then come back for you," he said to her.

"Did you find him?" she asked, looking amazed.

"Yes. He's tied up and there's no one to cut him loose. The horses are at the base of this hill."

"I'll go to the bottom of the slope."

"Stay up here."

"No, I can make my way down. Go and get those horses."

He shook his head in disapproval and set the dun down the slope. He didn't want to look back at her making her way unsteadily off the hill. He went after the saddled ponies, which were busy gathering grass through their bits. He soon had the dozen or so tied in a train, reins to saddle horn, and turned back to get Mary, who was already standing waiting at the base of the slope.

"Whew," she said, removing his hat and wiping her forehead on the back of her hand. "Did you get all of them?"

"All that are here."

"Where do I ride?"

"Up behind me. Here, give me your hand." She found the stirrup next, and was propelled by his lift onto the saddle behind him.

"I'll have to hold you to stay on," she said.

"No time for worrying about that."

"I guess not. Pee-yew. These clothes stink bad, don't they?"

"Least of my worries right now, Mary. Let's go show off their horses."

"Really?" Her small hands were clasped around his stomach and she pressed herself to his back.

"My plans exactly." He looked back over her at the long manes blowing in the wind. He had the breeds' horses. The attackers could plan to walk home. In fact, the breeds' camp, as he recalled, wasn't overrun with horse stock. They all might have to walk for a while.

19

Slocum made a wide berth of the wagons until he felt he was far enough north of them. The line of breed horses pranced and danced. Some of the stallions in the bunch squealed and acted up, but they came on.

Slocum began to circle back. The shots were less frequent, and he wondered how the wagon folks were holding out.

"What will we do next?" Mary asked, moving up on the back of the saddle and resetting her grasp around his stomach.

"I would like to rush through them and take the horses in with us."

"I can hang on."

"We may get shot at."

"Like Lane told me, we better live for today, and I know they need you in there to help them."

"Hang on then when I shout."

"I may squeeze you to death." She tightened her grasp on him.

He drove the ponies down the draw, hoping to be out of sight until the last minute. He wondered what to shout so the wagon folks would know he and Mary weren't breeds. No sense being shot by your own people.

"Need my hat back," he said. "They see a bareheaded man riding in, they might think I was a breed."

"Right. Can I scream too?"

"Loud as you want when we start."

He guided the dun up the hill, looking for a sniper. He saw none, and gave the loudest rebel yell he had. The horses, anticipating something, gathered up close, and he sent heels to the dun.

"Boo-ah-whoop!" she screamed, so loud it hurt his ears, but they were flying over the grass by then. He kept up his yelling, and her screams rang across the prairie. With the small Colt ready in his hand should a breed pop up, they closed in on the three wagons. At the last moment, they came to a sliding stop at the wagons.

"Grab the horse, boys," he shouted, swinging her down. "We've got them breeds afoot."

Mark, Luke, and the bareheaded Lane rushed out and began to secure and tie up the ponies. Then Lane rushed over and swept his wife up in his arms.

"Aw, Mary, thank God you're all right."

"Thanks to Slocum."

Slocum looked up at the gunpowder-blackened face of Mrs. Blair as she leaned out of the back of the wagon and peered at them. "Where have you two been all day?" Then she laughed, and the others did too.

Somewhere in the distance, Slocum heard another welcome sound. It was a train whistle blowing this time. He studied Mary, whose small red-rimmed eyes were closed, tears streaming down her face, and she was turned toward the sound of the whistle.

From beside the wagon, Slocum watched the breeds begin to melt away. Some shook their fists from the safety of the ridge; others dropped their pants in insult. No matter. They had given up their attack for the moment. And horseless, they had many miles to walk to get back to their camp.

"Are they gone for good?" Lane asked Slocum, scratching the thatch of graying hair on top of his head.

"No, because they can't risk us telling the authorities about their raid."

"How far is it to civilization?"

"I don't figure far. You heard the train."

"Yeah, sounded good. Dare we go find it?"

"We better, before Devereau and his breeds make a new plan."

"And Slocum, I'll repay you for bringing her back. Figured I'd never see her again."

"You don't owe me a thing."

"I do, and I will."

The wagons soon rolled. Mark herded the new horses with the rest of the loose stock at the rear, and Luther went out as the point guard. Slocum changed to a stout piebald stud from the breeds' ponies and let the spent dun trail along with the herd.

"Hope we find a stream soon," Mrs. Blair said to him in passing. "Poor Mary wants a bath so bad, says those clothes she's wearing are worse than a pile of dung."

"They aren't fresh-washed?"

"Oh, Slocum," she gushed. "I'm so glad she's safe, she could smell like a polecat and I'd hug her every chance I got."

He agreed, and glanced up front. Mary was back in her usual role, whip in hand, driving her teams. Still dressed in the filthy men's clothing, she had on a sunbonnet that hid her face and shaded her weak eyes, but she could crack that whip and the oxen knew who was boss. No wonder that Lane was so concerned about her return. He would have had to drive them himself. But Slocum felt a special admiration for her. Being handicapped by her poor eyesight didn't stop her.

In two hours, they found the railroad tracks, and the humming telegraph lines, shining like two silver threads in the sun. With nothing in sight they turned west, parallel to the rails, and headed toward the low red sunset in the late afternoon.

A flowing creek soon presented itself, and Lane called for them to stop. Slocum and the boys hobbled the ponies to keep them close and to make it hard for the breeds in a desperate raid to drive them off.

From the corner of his eye, he saw Mary and Mrs. Blair, leading her, head for the stream, going under the bridge for privacy. Mrs. Blair carried a towel and a fresh dress over one arm. They both talked like magpies, and though at the distance their words were not clear enough to decipher, he knew they had much to say to each other.

"I heard our stepmom say you chewed the rawhide from her wrists." Luther looked taken back by the notion.

"She couldn't reach the knife in my boot," Slocum explained.

"You have a knife in your boot?"

"Yes, I always carry one there. You never know when you'll need one."

"Barefooted, it wouldn't do much good," Luther said, flexing his dusty toes and laughing.

"You'll wear boots someday and pack an extra in them." He put his boot up on the wagon tongue and showed the boys the sheath sewn in the vamp.

"Packing that Colt in there too?"

"I did."

"Ever make you sore? I mean packing that gun in there too?"

"I can't count the times it saved my life, including today."

"Maybe someday . . ." Luther grinned and went off.

"We better post guards and dogs, right?" Lane said, gnawing on some jerky as he came up.

"Be best, the way I figure," Slocum said.

"I'll do it. Well, Mary's coming back all cleaned up. She sure hated them stinking clothes she had to wear, but she sure spoke good of you," Lane said.

"You have a wonderful wife. You're lucky."

"I have her because of you. Mary, you look radiant," Lane said to her as she came up.

"I smell much better anyway. I left those clothes down there. We decided they were too filthy to wash." Her words drew laughter from Mrs. Blair, who agreed.

The women cooked dried beans and used the last of their salt pork in it. Mrs. Dugan made sourdough biscuits in the Dutch oven, and in the twilight the wagon folks all ate and laughed in a lighthearted way. Slocum sat cross-legged in their circle and let some of the past day's tension drain from his body.

Slocum finished his food and offered the men cigars. Lane refused one, and so did the others. Slocum lit his and shook out the match. Then he leaned back, inhaled the smoke, and felt the nicotine relax him some.

"I ran out of chawing tobacco yesterday and said to myself, 'Lane, why don't you quit?' Tobacco won't grow up here and I'd have to buy it at some store."

"So you quit?" Slocum asked.

"Yeah, sure did."

"Did you want some when those breeds had you all pinned down earlier?"

"Worst in my life. But I promised the Lord, if he'd deliver me and bring Mary back unharmed, I'd never chew another pinch of it."

"Sounds to me like a reformed man."

"He chewed enough for two folks before, so he don't need any more," Blair said, and they all laughed.

Lane reached over and hugged Mary's shoulder. "I promised the Lord things before and always kept them. Ain't I, darling?"

"You're a man of your word, Lane."

"How true, how true. Slocum, what will you do in Montana?"

"A man named Lucas sent word that he needed me to drive some cattle for him. Why I was headed up here in the first place."

"You worked for him before?"

"I made some drives for him."

"You know we ain't got nothing to do up here," Lane began. "Our women and little ones would be safe enough at Billings, if you needed some hands."

"I may be too late for the job, but I would sure consider hiring you."

The others nodded, and he finished his cigar, said his pleasantries, and retired to his bedroll away from the wagons. Bone tired, he pulled off his boots. He knew the dogs were tied out, and he had told the men when they needed him for guard duty, to come wake him.

His eyes popped open to the dark of night. Was it time for his guard duty? Then he saw her standing over him. She dropped to her knees and leaned forward.

"It's me, Mary," she whispered. "We don't have much time, but I want a very big favor from you." She lifted his blankets and slipped in the bedroll beside him. Her small eyes avoided his, and she looked at the stars. "Lane and I won't ever have a child." She shook her head and wet her lips. "Slocum—I—we want yours."

"Does he know?" In dismay, Slocum rose up and looked around. She pulled him back down.

"He knows. I'm sorry I can't give you much time to think about it."

"He knows?" He raised up enough to look at her face.

"Yes. How else would I have found you out here? Now, do I need to take off all my clothes?" Obviously, she was undoing the front of her dress.

He rested his forehead on hers. "I can't promise you—"

She put the fingers of one hand on his lips to silence him, and with the other put his hand on her right breast. Her fingers fumbled with his shirt buttons, and he softly fondled the globe-shaped breast. *Felicia, you were wrong. She has great ones.*

She undid his pants and pushed them down. He rose up to help her, then kicked them off. Her small fingers closed around his manhood. He rose and moved on top of her, his knees between her short legs. At this point, he discovered she wore no underwear. His heartbeat increased. Her anxious hand pumping on his shaft had turned it hard enough for his entry. He moved in and smiled down on her when she gasped at his intrusion.

He found the way was swollen, and wondered if his efforts to go deeper were hurting her, but she pulled him down on top of her. His hips ached with the pleasure of his discovery. The further they went, the more excited she became, raising her hips for his deepest probe. He discovered, reaching back to squeeze one side of her butt, how small she was.

Then they entered a seesaw battle of deep hard-fought efforts toward each other. Slocum felt the head of his dick swell to balloon-sized proportions, and then it exploded. His brain swirled, and he had trouble keeping his braced arms from collapsing and crushing her under his body.

He managed to fall off to the side, and lay there out of breath and spent. She cupped his face in her small hands and kissed him. In a second, she was up dressing.

He watched her silhouette as she made her way across the camp without a misstep. *Liar, liar. You found your own way out here.* He closed his sore eyes and lay down on his side. As he slipped off to sleep again, he was still making love to Mary.

20

The army patrol came with the Stars and Stripes and their guidon flag flapping in the afternoon wind. Slocum reined up the dun and considered them as he rubbed his whisker-bristled mouth with the palm of his hand. Usually he didn't find all that much to cheer about seeing blue soldier boys riding up, but he did this time.

He let Lane tell the captain in charge about the breeds and their attack on the wagons. A black-whiskered man, the lanky officer thanked them and took his leave, after promising that the breeds would be brought to justice. Slocum turned in the saddle and watched the yellow-striped legs going southeast, and wondered what they would find at the breeds' camp.

The military should put an end to the problem caused by the breeds. He twisted back at the crack of Mary's whip. The wagons were headed west again, and he felt relieved. His worst enemy was being taken care of, at least the worst one he had right now.

Where were the Abbott brothers lurking? He hadn't left them much to track him with since he'd left the Rose Bud. But he would have to have all his senses about him. In a few days, he would be in Billings. Civilization meant not only that the Abbott brothers could be hanging around, but that some other bounty hunter might be lurking in the wings. He

would have to keep his back to the wall and find Johnny
Lucas, for whatever he was up to.

That night, Mary awoke him again. He raised up and
looked around suspiciously. Nothing looked out of place.
With a scowl he frowned at her. Already on her back in his
bedroll, she had her dress unbuttoned, and pulled him on top
of her.

"I need to be sure," she said, and began to undo his shirt.

Three days later, they came off the long grade and de-
scended into Billings, a cluster of false-front buildings and
tents along the Northern Pacific tracks and the Yellowstone
River. Lane selected a place to camp on the riverbank at the
edge of town. Slocum shook everyone's hands, and accepted
their gratitude graciously. When he came to Mary, she looked
at the ground.

"I never knew a man like you—but I won't ever forget
your gnawing on that rawhide to get me loose." She never
opened her eyes, simply reached out, hugged him, then rested
her face on his vest for a long moment.

He wouldn't forget her either for some time. When all the
good-byes were said, he started to mount the dun.

"You need any hands on that drive, we'll be here," Lane
reminded him.

Slocum said that he would keep them in mind, thanked
him, waved, and headed for town.

He put his dun in the first livery. Then he started checking
the row of saloons on the right-hand side of the street. Lucas
would be in one of them, playing cards, if he wasn't broke.
The first one held nothing but drunks loitering around, and
he didn't stay. He pushed his way through the batwing doors
of a fancier saloon, and wandered back to the poker-playing
area.

"Looking for Johnny Lucas," he said openly, and drew the
scornful gazes of several fancy-dressed cardplayers.

"Try the Gold Dust."

"Better yet, look over at that Chinese whorehouse," another
said, busy pulling his discards. "He's got him some new gal
over there."

"Yeah, and he's probably up there this time of day," one

of the older men said, checking his gold watch.

"Thanks." Lucas was still in town. Good news, but did he still need cattle driven somewhere? Slocum headed for the Gold Dust next.

The Gold Dust Saloon's bartender sent him to Sue Ling's place. Slocum was breathing hard from climbing the grade uphill when he reached the false-fronted tent. He gazed back over Billings, with the swirling smoke of cooking fires in the air, and caught his breath.

A small Oriental girl ushered him inside, and he could see the walls of the place were canvas. The midday sun filtered through the cloth and gave the girl and the furnishings a yellow cast. She showed him to a sofa and bowed after telling him that Sue Ling would be right with him.

"Ah, there you are," a pert-looking Chinese woman in a red silk kimono said, coming into the room. "What kind of girl you want? Have plenty pretty ones."

"No girl. Johnny Lucas. Lucas here?" He removed his hat for her.

"Oh, yes, but—" She glanced toward the canvas door that led to the rear, then back at Slocum. "He may not be able to come out here—right now."

"I can wait here if you don't mind. I've come a couple hundred miles to see him at his request."

"Who should I say is here?"

"Slocum."

"Have chair, Mr. Slocum. Could I have young lady come and entertain you?"

"No."

"I will have girl bring you hot tea. No charge." She smiled and nodded. "Excuse, please?"

"Certainly."

The slender derriere in the silk wrapper disappeared through the doorway. He dropped on the stuffed couch. Soon a young girl came with a tray containing a red-gold pot of tea, and handed him a cup and saucer.

He nodded, and held the cup for her to fill. She wore little more than a thin cotton shift, and after she filled the cup, she knelt on the floor as if ready to refill it.

"Need sugar?" she asked.

He nodded, and she set the tray down. With a small silver spoon, she scooped some sugar from a bowl, placed it in his cup of steaming brew, and stirred it. She waited for him to sip it.

"Is good?"

"Fine," he said, and she sat back on her heels. "You can sit on the furniture," he said, feeling very uncomfortable with her at his feet.

"You like me to sit by you?" She blinked her slanted eyes at him.

"Fine," he said, anxious to have her off the floor.

She swept the gown under her legs and sat down beside him. He glanced over at her, with her hands folded in her lap, and then looked at the sun-glowing ceiling. Why, she looked to be twelve years old. Man, he could recall his first tumble in bed with an Oriental girl. Come to think of it, he decided, his first one probably wasn't much older than this one.

"Can do things to please you?" she asked very meekly.

"Yes," he said. "Sit there."

"Slocum!" He heard Lucas's booming voice coming from the rear. Dressed in a tailored business suit, the man filled the doorway with a gold chain spanning his vast waist and a nearly naked Oriental girl under his arm.

She clutched a sheet to cover her obvious nakedness. Lucas strode over and stuck out a great ham of hand.

"Boy, I thought you would never get here."

"I wondered a few times myself."

"Hey, grab that girl over there and come back. We're having a little fun back there." Lucas tossed his head toward the rear. The prostitute with him at last managed to wrap herself up better in the sheet, and crowded close to him, so he closed his arm over her.

"I want to clean up and do a few things," Slocum told him. "What did you need me for?"

"Hell, honey, I can tell he don't want any pussy right now." Lucas dug out some money and put the bills in her hand. "Me and him got to talk some business. You run along and Daddy will be back." He swatted her on the butt and sent her toward the rear door.

"Let's go talk." Lucas indicated the front door, and Slocum took the lead.

They found a table in the back of the Gold Dust Saloon that was private enough to talk at during the midday slack in business, and Lucas ordered a bottle of rye whiskey. Slocum took the tumbler that Lucas half filled and considered it.

"I've got a moneymaking sumbitch." Lucas lowered his voice. "I've got beef coming from Illinois by rail and guaranteed—" He looked around to be certain they were alone. "Guaranteed to make me rich."

"How's that? What are you doing with them?"

"Selling them to the damn Injuns. The agents anyway. Got me this one agent is taking ten cars of cattle at twenty cents on the hoof."

"What are they costing?"

"That's the good part. They're delivering them for nine cents at the railhead to me."

"How in the hell are they doing that?"

Lucas settled his big frame back in the chair. "Gawdamned if I know."

Slocum shook his head. They had to be real culls at that price. But rail freight and all . . . It didn't add up. They had to be stolen.

"I met this businessman in a fancy hotel in Chicago," Lucas said. "He saw I was from the West and we struck up a conversation. Next thing I'm talking to moneymen, bankers, and more fancy dudes than I can shake a stick at."

Lucas handed him an expensive cigar. "They left the marketing out here to me. I wired them after I talked to this agent, and said I had them sold for twenty cents a pound. Course, I've got to split the difference with them for putting up the money."

Slocum considered the hand-rolled smoke, amazed at Lucas's good fortune. He licked the tube with the tip of his tongue, and wondered some more about Lucas's deal. It didn't sound right. Too much money. But why should it worry him? He was hiring on as a drover, not a partner.

"Then what do you need me for?" Slocum asked.

"I need them drove from the railhead to the reservation. All these crazy bastards up here are either sodbusters, or wouldn't know a steer's butt from a chicken's ass. I need a trail-driving boss and a crew."

"No cowboys up here?"

"Hell, no, they all must be back in Texas. Now everyone ships cattle up here by rail. Besides, the damn Powder River Country, south of here, is stuffed plumb full of them wild injuns. I've been about frantic. Didn't know what I'd do if you didn't show. But thank Gawd you're finally here."

"What reservation do these cattle go to?" Slocum asked.

"The Rose Bud. Wounded Knee Agency. Agent's name is McFaye."

21

Slocum was headed for the livery. The rye whiskey had settled him a little, but he wondered how he would drive eight hundred head of cattle from the rail to the agency with some Kentucky farmers. How good would those piebald horses of the breeds be for a remuda? They'd need a chuck wagon or a pack string. And a cook? Damn, Lucas had been in Billings long enough to know how little help was available, and for a cattle drive it would be damn tight. Mining jobs further west had drawn off most of the men who wanted to work.

When a blanket-wrapped Indian seated on the porch of the store cleared his throat at Slocum's approach, Slocum blinked at him. The buck rose and went into the space between the building with a nod at Slocum. Slocum paused and frowned, looked up and down the street, and not seeing any threat, stepped off the boardwalk and entered the space.

"Snow Bear? What in the hell are you doing here?" he asked the Indian.

"Come to help you."

"Lord, I don't need—yes, I do. But whatever possessed you to come here?"

"I go and look for Spirit Woman. Then I see you and say maybe she sent me to help you."

"How is everyone at the agency?"

Snow Bear shook his head. "Soon they are supposed to have beef for us."

"I know. I'm going to deliver it."

"Good, I can help you."

"You haven't seen those bounty men again?"

"Ones with the Nez Percé horse?"

"Right."

"No, have not seen them or the Spirit Woman."

"She ain't in Billings?"

Snow Bear smiled, then shook his head. "I will find her one day."

"I know you will. Where is your horse?"

"A Cheyenne woman keeps him for me by her lodge near the river."

"Good. I'll get my horse and ride out to my camp. You can come along. I need to make up an outfit to drive those cattle to the Rose Bud."

They rode double, and went to pick up Snow Bear's bay horse. Slocum grinned as the old man told the attractive Cheyenne woman thanks. There might be snow on the mountain, but Snow Bear still had much fire in him. They rode on to Lane's camp.

"Ah, Slocum," Lane said when they reached his camp. "Who's your friend?"

"Snow Bear, a powerful medicine man for the Sioux nation."

"What can we do for you two?"

"I need to hire some drovers with saddle horses and a chuck wagon. But we'll need a pair of mules to pull it. Oxen are too slow."

"What are you doing with all this?" Lane asked with a grin.

By then everyone from the camp was gathered to listen.

"I need to deliver eight hundred steers to the Rose Bud reservation for starters," Slocum said.

"What's it pay?" Lane asked, showing Slocum and Snow Bear to some blankets on the ground.

"Dollar a day and found. Plus a bonus of five bucks a man if we deliver on time."

"Any doubt about that?" Lane asked.

"Hurricanes, tornadoes, rattlesnakes, mean Indians, and lots of country to cover."

Lane looked around. "Guess you heard the man. What's the vote?"

"We go," came the chorus.

"Hold it!" Slocum held out his hands. "This ain't a family affair. I can't look after women folks, children, and get those cattle there."

"My wife can stay here with Mrs. Blair. Close as she is, she sure don't need to be out there," Dugan said. "They can keep the kids right here."

Heads bobbed, and then Mary came forward. "I can drive mules, did it at home."

"I don't know, Mary." Slocum dropped his chin. A near-blind woman driving some half-broke mules with all their supplies in the wagon seemed too chancy to him, and she'd have to go ahead each day and make the next camp.

"We can find her a helper somewhere," Lane said, satisfied that would solve Slocum's concerns.

"You boys ever drive any cattle?" Slocum finally asked.

Mark and Luther nodded. Hell, they meant the loose stock for the wagon train. The others looked as if they were waiting for him to say more.

"They're bringing longhorns. Six-year-old steers, been raised by monkeys in the brush. They'll gore you if they catch you off your horse on your feet. They'll stampede for no damn reason at all. They're spooky as ghosts. Half will want to run away, the others poke along."

"Slocum," Lane begun. "We never made a wagon train before and you seen us. Well, you helped us get here. We can drive any damn longhorns you got. Besides, we're broke flat as a flitter and need the work."

Everyone agreed. From behind her sunbonnet, Mary, standing beside the wagon wheel, smiled confidently as if it was all set. Slocum closed his eyes. Lucas had promised him a hundred and fifty bucks for his part if he managed to get all the steers there and on time.

"When do we start?" Lane asked.

"In the morning, I'll order the supplies and have them on

the dock of Wyman's Store by noon. Meanwhile, I'll find a team of mules and harness for you. We better run, Snow Bear."

"We'll have an empty wagon at the store in town by noon," Lane promised.

"Day after that," Slocum said, "we leave for this railhead where they are going to unload them." That said, he swung up in the saddle.

"Slocum, thanks. You won't be disappointed," Lane promised him.

He saluted them and rode out with Snow Bear.

The supplies were easy. Slocum knew what he wanted, and got the young clerks busy gathering it. Snow Bear stood back, wrapped in his blanket like some cigar-store Indian. When one of the young men asked about him in a surly manner, Slocum dismissed him with; "That's my grandfather."

"Any of you know of a team of mules for sale?" Slocum asked, signing for all his purchases. He had foodstuff like rice, flour, baking soda, raisins, sugar, salt, and pepper. Then horseshoes, nails, ropes, some extra blankets, a few bottles of whiskey for medicinal purposes, leather for repairs, and a couple of cases of canned tomatoes and peaches. Also four new rifles and four hundred rounds of ammo. Lucas would need to make plenty of money on these cattle to afford his hands and their keep.

"Grandfather." Snow Bear sniffed when they were outside.

"Too damn complicated to tell them," Slocum explained.

Snow Bear nodded in agreement and they went across the street to the livery. The man in charge sent them to another wagon yard to look for a team of mules. Slocum found a pair of stout ones there, but wanted to see them driven. He had the man harness them. The whites showing around their eyes made him believe that they were too wild for a near-blind woman to drive.

When they were hooked up, the stable helper drove them around the yard, but Slocum could see the reins were wrapped around the man's wrist, and the mules would have dragged him off if he hadn't hurried.

"Real Missouri mules," the livery man bragged.

"Look pretty damn salty to me," Slocum complained.

"Couple days' hard work and they'll drop in place like babies."

"That's why you have them for sale. They were too tame for the last fella?"

"Mister, good sound mules are damn hard to find. The army's using all they can buy. At a hundred bucks for the team and harness, they're a real bargain."

Slocum hugged his arms. If it was anyone besides Mary who was going to drive them, he wouldn't worry. But a near-blind woman had no business with these flighty mules. He nodded to Snow Bear to join him.

"What do you think?" Slocum asked.

Snow Bear nodded his head slowly in approval.

"Grandfather and I'll take them," Slocum said to the livery man. "John Lucas, who is up at that Chinese whorehouse, will pay you for them."

"I know him. Sign here." The man held out the paper and gave Slocum a pencil. "You driving them out of here?"

"No." Slocum gave the animals one more hard skeptical look. He hoped they would do, and signed his name. "I'll lead them off my horse," he added.

"Tie the lines up, Harry," the man said to his helper. "I need a hoodlum for the cook wagon. There a boy around here needs work?"

"What'll you pay?"

"Two bits a day if he'll work, and found."

"Aye, there's a boy called Garnett around here. I'll send him to see yeah. He'll fit your bill, mister, and you can whup his ass if he don't."

"He your boy?"

"Naw, some draggings. Think his mother's a whore that went onto the goldfields without him. God knows who's his father."

"Send him to our camp on the river."

"I'll do it. Hey, what kinda Injun is he?" The man jerked a thumb at Snow Bear.

"Abasinennin, I think," Slocum said.

"Hell, I've heard of them."

On his dun, Slocum took the rope leads of the spooky-acting mules, and wondered for a moment if they would climb in the saddle with him. Or if they might drag him and the dun off across the prairie. He was unsure what they would do next.

"I think all those people you called me died with the Blackfeet," Snow Bear said, riding in close.

"Hell, he didn't need to know any more than that." Slocum forced the spooky mules past a double wagon hitch of several oxen in the street. They would sure be a handful.

When Slocum and Snow Bear rode into their camp, Lane came out and surveyed the mules. He walked around them without a word.

"Young?" he said, meaning their age.

"Never mouthed them, but they looked young enough," Slocum said.

Lane walked up, peeled the near mule's lip back, and nodded. "Threes or fours."

"Can we get them so Mary can drive them?" Slocum asked.

Lane looked hard at the pair. "Yeah. We may not be cowboys but we can damn sure handle mules."

Slocum dropped out of the saddle and drew a deep breath. One problem solved. He led the dun down to the Yellowstone and let him drink. He would be glad to have this operation on the road.

"Will you eat some food we have ready?" Mrs. Blair asked him.

"If you have enough?"

"We have plenty. Tell your medicine man to come too."

"We will be right up there." He waited for the woman to get beyond hearing, and turned back to Snow Bear, who was squatted on the ground. "We going to make this cattle drive work?"

Snow Bear's lips pursed together, and he gave Slocum an unconcerned nod of approval.

Slocum washed his hands in the cold river water, and then stood up, drying them on the sides of his pants. "That's settled. Let's go to eat, Grandfather."

"Hmm, have a new name."

22

Slocum had his final visit with Lucas in the Chinese house of ill repute, and thanked him, but declined the man's invitation to enjoy some choice imported flesh at Lucas's expense. Everything was set. The cattle would arrive in five days at a siding called Manning Dakota Territory. They needed to have them at the Wounded Knee Agency in two weeks, and with plenty of weight still on them.

Sitting on the edge of the bed, dressed in a silk robe, Lucas blew a mouthful of cigar smoke in the air. Then he refilled his glass with whiskey. Slocum refused any more. He still had half a glass. He raised the tumbler to the man's toast.

"To making some money!" said Lucas.

"Yes," Slocum agreed, and they clinked glasses together.

Lucas's concubine, seated beside him, wrapped herself tighter in the sheet and tucked her small bare legs under her. Slocum figured that the man never let her dress.

"I'll be there when they weigh them, but if I'm delayed, you can be my agent and weigh them."

Slocum nodded. The smell of ginger and other spices was too strong in the tent. The afternoon sun shone on the canvas roof, and the sides of the room had no windows for ventilation.

"See you," Lucas said, and pulled her around on his lap. "Here, darlin', stand up and show him what he's missing."

"Look," he said to Slocum, who had reached the curtained doorway.

He turned back and saw the nymph of a girl standing there like Eve. Slocum nodded. "Pretty enough." He went out in the hallway.

He couldn't get out in the fresh air fast enough. When he reached the front flap and stepped outside, Snow Bear stood up and looked at him.

"They different than white or Indian women?" he asked, indicating the tent.

"No, all the same," Slocum said. And they both laughed, mounted up, and headed for the business district. Slocum recognized the familiar wagon parked at the store.

Lane, with his boys as outriders, had driven the wagon and mules to town for the supplies, and Slocum stopped to talk to them.

"How did they do coming here?" he asked Lane, who was packing sacks of beans and flour up the board ramp.

The man paused and then smiled. "They are kinda cautious, but they'll be fine by the time we get to that railhead in Dakota."

Slocum scowled at the new information. Lucas had only allowed them five days of travel time. The cattle would be there. He had no time for breaking mules.

"Hell, Mary will be driving them before we get there," Lane said, and ducked to enter the wagon.

"I hope so," Slocum said, and tied his horse to the hitch rack. They had an hour worth of loading ahead.

The boy they called Garnett waited for them in camp. When he stood up, Slocum saw the boy was cross-eyed. His heart sunk as he dismounted. How could a cross-eyed boy and near-blind women ever—too late to do a damn thing about it.

"You must be Garnett?" he asked.

The boy cocked his head sideways, as if to see him, and nodded.

"You ever helped a camp cook before?" Slocum could smell him by this time. He reeked like a garbage can.

"No, ah, sir," the boy lisped. "But I worked in kitchens, ah, washing dishes and things."

Besides selling him wild mules, the livery man had found him a boy with definite problems; cockeyed, a speech impediment, and in need of a serious bath.

"You ever take a bath?" Slocum asked.

"Some, ah, times."

"I'll get you some soap and a towel," he said, and started for the women, who were busy cooking.

"Our cook's helper needs a bath," Slocum announced.

"Heavens, yes. We been smelling him all afternoon. Here." Mrs. Blair issued Slocum both soap and a towel. "And have him wear my husband's shirt. It will do for a robe until we can wash those filthy clothes of his."

"Sorry," Slocum said privately to her. "I had no idea."

"Aw, some soap, water, and clean clothes and he won't be half bad."

"I hope not," Slocum said, then handed everything to Garnett and pointed the bedraggled youth toward the river. "Use lots of that soap too," he said after him.

That afternoon, Garnett began to split wood with a hand ax for Mary. She immediately began to show him things to do, and Slocum hoped he didn't chop himself. Slocum was busy with resetting the shoes on the dun. Snow Bear squatted on the ground and surveyed the entire operation.

Close to dusk, Lane came and told them to wash up for supper. Slocum straightened, with his back complaining, and set down the last hoof.

"I have watched all day. These people are farmers, yet they plant nothing?" Snow Bear asked.

"They have not found land to farm yet."

"This land here won't do?"

"It isn't theirs to farm."

Snow Bear shook his head. "But they took this land from the Lakota. Now it is theirs, right?"

"No, the government has laws. Each piece of ground belongs to individuals or the government. They can go out there on government lands and stake land and live on it, and it will be theirs someday." Slocum rinsed his hands in the river and flung them dry.

"Someday they will farm?"

"That's what they did in Kentucky."

"Why did they leave Kentucky?"

"Why did you leave the Rose Bud?"

"To look for the Spirit Woman."

"Maybe they're looking for theirs too."

"Oh, I never thought they had lost their god."

"Maybe they look for it too."

"I understand," Snow Bear said, and they went back to camp to eat supper.

Slocum noticed Snow Bear could not resist questioning these white men, and when supper was over the man began to ask about Kentucky. Lane described it as a green country with rain and rivers.

"Why did you come out here?" Snow Bear asked.

"Too damn many people moving in."

Slocum grinned when Snow Bear nodded soberly.

Lane drove the mules the first day. Mary sat beside him on the seat. Garnett rode a broke horse and followed the wagon. The men herded the breed horses for extras, and they all set out to the meadowlarks' shrill song. Women and children waved until they were out of sight.

Slocum set the pace and they trotted. By dark, when they made camp, the mules had lost most of their unruly fire, and Lane bragged on them. Mary sent her helper off gathering buffalo chips with the others, and started her fire.

With all the stock hobbled, Slocum scheduled only one guard, and that was rotated every two hours. He and Snow Bear threw down their blankets after her fine meal. Slocum wanted some real meat, and the next day he planned to find it out there. Lucas's cattle-drive business was all in a jumble inside his head. The last thing that Slocum thought about before he closed his eyes was the naked Chinese girl standing by the man's side.

He brought in an antelope the next day. Mary and her helper quickly skinned it and turned it into eatable products. Everyone bragged on the tasty treat at supper, and Slocum agreed. However, his crew could eat one whole antelope each day, and they were hard to find.

"Can we get another one tomorrow," he asked Snow Bear as they sat eating supper.

Snow Bear nodded. Slocum finished the meat on the rib bone and tossed it away. If the medicine man was right, then they'd have more meat the next day too.

On the third day, Mary drove the wagon and Garnett, who was not a horse rider, became her point man on the seat. Slocum drew a deep breath and hoped for the best. He needed no one hurt, not to mention the loss of his supplies. They left in a rattle of wagon wheels and harness without a hitch. Snow Bear rode off to the south, and by noontime Slocum began to wonder about the man and where he had gone.

Slocum rode up to a high place and used his telescope, but caught no sign of the medicine man. Snow Bear was capable enough to take care of himself. But Slocum simply didn't want him hurt, or to need help with no one to go to him. Snow Bear didn't appear at supper, and afterwards Slocum sat cross-legged, and was smoking a cigar when he heard a horse returning.

"Is that Snow Bear?" Mary called out.

"I think so."

"Tell him I saved a plate of food for him."

"Thanks, I will."

Snow Bear dropped heavily from the horse. He squatted down and surveyed his back trail, bathed in the blood of the sunset.

"You got followers," he said to Slocum.

"Breeds?"

Snow Bear nodded.

"How many?"

"Six or seven."

"They after us?"

"Devereau asked me if I knew you."

"What did you say?"

"I said, why should I know a white eyes?"

"What did he say?"

"Said he should have killed you when he had you."

"I thought the army might have got him by this time."

"I think he had a running battle with them and barely got away at night."

"He knows I'm out here?" Slocum could hardly fathom how the man would know that.

"Yes. His woman saw you in Billings and learned that you are going after cattle."

"Felicia?"

"Yes, that is her."

"Mary has some food for you. Go get it. I'll think on this awhile."

He had a better force this time. Only one woman, and she could fight like a man. Devereau would not kidnap her so easily this time. She had much more savvy. Still, Slocum didn't dare delay getting to Mann and the cattle unloading.

Perhaps they could outrun the breeds. To his way of thinking, they could reach the yards in one more hard day's push. Perhaps they could camp there and defend themselves better at the cattle pens than out in the open. There was not much cover where they were at.

"You have a good plan?" Snow Bear asked, sitting down with his heaping plate of food.

"One that we're going to try."

23

"You see them yet?" Lane asked as the crew lounged behind the pens and Slocum used his telescope to scan the country.

"Nothing. They won't come until dark."

"Where did Snow Bear go?"

"No telling. He may be out there talking to them about what they're going to do when they attack us. They don't know that he comes and tells us everything he hears."

"All that smoke today. Indians sending signals, wasn't it? They were pretty busy. You understand it?"

"No," Slocum said. "I've wished all day that Snow Bear was here. He'd know the meaning of it all."

"You and him sure are good friends."

"Snow Bear's a good man. I'd trust him with my life. He'll help us if he can."

"We have those four new repeaters, ammunition you bought, plus our own guns. I think we could hold off an army."

"We may have to."

Mary came around with a granite coffeepot and metal cups. "You two want some?" she asked, crouching down beside the two men.

"Sure do," Slocum said, and collapsed the scope. Nothing to see anyway. He took a cup from her.

"You can pour," she said, and set the pot on the ground. "I might burn you."

"Fine. Garnett working out?" he asked, filling Lane's cup, then his own.

"He's good enough help. Says he sees twice as much as most people because he sees double. I wish I had half of his vision."

"You do good, Mary," Lane bragged, and Slocum agreed.

"That don't mean if I could see better it won't be better."

"That's right," her husband said.

"When will the cattle arrive?" she asked.

"Tomorrow, I guess," Slocum said.

"Good. Then we can move on."

"You don't like it here?"

"No shade, no trees. I like to listen to the river run."

"It won't happen up here for sure."

She found the coffeepot with the toe of her foot, then caught the handle. "I'll keep it warm on the fire, in case you two want more."

"Thanks, Mary," Lane said after her.

She acknowledged she'd heard him, and moved off.

"She does lots for what she can do, but she's a lot of responsibility," Lane said, holding his cup to his mouth and pausing as if considering the matter. "She's stubborn as a damn mule when she sets her mind to it."

"Lots of grit in her."

"Too much at times." Lane said, and then sipped on his coffee.

The two boys were herding the horses close by. Slocum didn't want them out of his sight. That would give the breeds a chance to separate them from him and the others. So far it had all gone well. If the cattle ever arrived, they could get the drive under way.

Another distant column of smoke streaked the southern sky. Slocum studied it. Where in the hell was Snow Bear at? Was it friendly smoke or unfriendly? He had no way to know. If the damn breeds knew his business so well, they could lay in wait anywhere to ambush him between the pens and the agency. A hundred and fifty or so miles of hell.

The day dragged on. Slocum rode out to the south and found no sign of breeds. The horse tracks he saw were all old, and might have been made by wild horses. Then he swung east, figuring they might think he wouldn't check on anything over there. Nothing out of place, no sign. But another column of smoke marked the azure sky.

Who in the hell was putting up all the signals? He considered riding south to discover the source, but knew the smoke was farther away than it looked, perhaps eight or ten miles away. Besides, if it wasn't a trap to lure him into an ambush, the smoke maker would be long gone before Slocum found the place. He turned the dun in a long trot and headed for camp.

"See anything?" Blair asked, meeting him at the side of the corrals. The horses and mules were penned inside, and the Lane boys sauntered over to join him.

"Never seen anything out of place. Any of you see anything?" Slocum asked them.

They all shook their heads.

"You figure out the smoke?" Blair asked, and the others waited for Slocum's answer.

"No idea." Slocum looked to the south, but there were no tall black streaks in sight. Maybe Snow Bear could explain it, if he ever showed up. Slocum stripped the saddle off the dun, and let him graze the short grass through the bits.

"Been a real long day, boys," he said to them. "No telling, we may not see the breeds and they may not find us. But we need to keep up our guard. Cattle arrive in the morning, or should by Lucas's schedule."

"We leaving then?"

Slocum nodded. "We can move them to a creek south of here and see how they're going to drive. If they stampede on us, we can let them run a ways, tire them out, and then stop them in this open country easier than we can later in the reservation breaks."

A bullet shattered the top board of the corral.

"Get down," Slocum shouted, and everyone took cover.

He hit the grass, and tried to figure out where the shooter

was located. Then he saw Mary busy bending over her kettles and pots on the fire.

"Mary! Get down!" he shouted.

The next round clanged off a kettle close to her. She was down on her hands and knees in a flash, headed for under the wagon, where Garnett lay with his hands covering his ears.

"Where are they?" Lane asked, on his belly a few yards away.

"A long ways off. Figure they've either got a buffalo or a needle gun and are shooting to pin us down," Slocum said.

"Doing a damn good job of it."

"Everyone stay down. They're taking potshots," Slocum said, anxious to locate the gunman out there and stop him.

"But my food—" Mary protested.

"Mary Lane, you stay right there!" her husband ordered. "We've got more food. There ain't but one of you."

On the ground under the wagon, she flipped the sunbonnet back, and Slocum saw the grin on her face. It was the first time he'd ever heard Lane say as much to his wife, but the man was serious and it pleased her.

A meadowlark sounded off. Horses in the corrals anxiously shuffled around and snorted in the dust. The afternoon wind picked up, and Slocum wondered where the sniper was at. He managed to slither across to his saddlebags, and drew out the scope. He wanted the shooter eliminated before dark. It was close to five in the afternoon, and the sun wouldn't go down for four more hours. Plenty of time to get rid of the nuisance.

A half hour passed with no more shots. The men grew restless. Mary had gone in a crouch to stir her food, and now hurried back to cover, grumbling out loud about the worthless unseen shooter.

"Reckon he's still out there?" Lane asked.

"We need a gun cleaning rod and an old hat," Slocum said. "And we'll see if he is."

"How?"

"Hold the hat up and when he shoots at it, I'll be looking for the gun smoke in my scope and we can pinpoint him."

"Mark, give me that hat of yours. A bullet hole in it might help its looks," Lane said to his son.

His words drew nervous laughter from the others all down in the grass behind the pen.

Blair furnished a cleaning rod. The attention of the crew was on what would happen next.

"Raise it slow-like until it clears the fence," Slocum said. He readied his scope. "Then everyone look quick for the gun smoke and get down before he reloads."

Lying on his back, Lane carefully raised the hat up, using the rod, until it was up to the top rail. The bullet tore through it and sent it spinning away.

"There!" Mark pointed. "He's southwest. See the smoke?"

Slocum saw the sniper for the first time through the lens. A breed up on his knees busy reloading his rifle's breech. Slocum knew none of their long guns would reach him. But the thought that one shooter could keep them pinned down like this drew his ire.

"What should we do?" Lane asked, crawling on his belly until he was beside Slocum.

"Eliminate that breed out there."

"How?"

"When the next train passes, we'll have a horse ready to ride west on this side of the train for cover, so he can't see the rider, then circle in behind him."

"I want to do it," the boy Luther volunteered enthusiastically.

"You ever killed a man?" Slocum asked.

"No."

"It ain't all that easy, and we don't need to give this shooter a chance. Secondly, you can't tell. There may be the whole gang out there under the hill."

"I'll go," Lane said. "I can damn sure kill him."

"You've got a wife and these boys to think about." Slocum glassed the breed again. He could see the man's hat now where he lay in the windswept grass on the ridge.

"They can take care of themselves," Lane said. "Besides, they'll need you to show them how to drive those cattle to Rose Bud."

"All right, but tell Mary what you're up to."

"You'll listen for the train?" Lane asked, raising up on his hands and knees.

"We will," Slocum said, and the others nodded as Lane ran for the wagon in a low crouch.

When Lane was under it, Slocum turned back with his scope. He could at least see when the man was taking aim. But the sniper was doing nothing when he scoped him again.

"Keep low and toss my saddle on the dun," Slocum said to Mark. "And get ready to get down when I say so. I can see the shooter."

Slocum studied the spot in the scope. He heard the saddle land on the dun and the leathers and cinches clap. Luther had gone to help Mark, and the two boys' heavy breathing was louder than the wind.

"We've got him saddled! He ready to shoot yet?" the breathless Luther asked, back at Slocum's elbow.

"Train's coming," Blair said down the line.

"Yeah, I hear it too," Dugan added.

"Lane, come and get ready to ride," Slocum said.

"Be careful," Mary said after him.

The farmer soon joined Slocum. "I'll ride west with the train for a shield, then cut south and come in behind him." He made signs with his hands.

"If there is a whole band of them, you come right back here," Slocum said. He needed him back in one piece.

"I will."

"No, I mean come *right* back here," Slocum said, and Lane nodded, then took the dun out of the pen and behind them.

The wailing moan of the train whistle drew closer. It wouldn't stop at this siding, so Lane needed to mount fast and ride like the wind.

"I'll get him," Lane promised.

Slocum nodded. The man held one of the new .44-40's in his hand. "Got plenty of shells?"

"A pocketful."

"That enough?"

"Where I was raised they loaded an old cap-and-ball rifle and told you make it count for a squirrel or bring one down with rocks." Lane smiled, ready to mount up.

The chugging and whistle of the train drew closer, and Slocum checked on the breed. Still out there.

Soon the ground under Slocum began to vibrate, and the engine came rushing by. They waved to the engineer. Lane mounted the dun and headed west in a race with the train. The rattle of the freight cars and clack of the wheels filled the air. It caused the horses to nervously mill about the pens. Then the thundering hooves of the dun were gone, and so was Lane. The caboose came by, and soon was gone too.

Slocum refocused on the sniper. The sharp smell of burning coal was still in his nostrils from the locomotive. The breed sniper was sitting up. Slocum could make out his unblocked hat and leather shirt. The dazzling late afternoon sun shone off the fancy beadwork on the man's blouse.

An hour passed, and a red-tailed hawk passed overhead, making lazy circles in search of his dinner. Unfettered by the strong wind, the bird of prey continued circling. In Slocum's frequent checks with the telescope, the breed still sat cross-legged out there with the rifle over his lap.

Then Slocum saw him stiffen and spill sideways. In the distance Slocum heard the delayed report of the rifle. Then the familiar hat came into his lens aboard his dun. Lane dismounted, swept up the man's rifle, and remounted the dun in a circle.

"Boys, get armed. He's bringing in company on his heels," Slocum shouted. A new rifle and a box of cartridges in hand, Slocum rushed around the corral and knelt on the side of the tracks to be ready. Lane had a good head start on the half-dozen breeds whipping their runty horses after him.

Slocum levered a shell in the chamber. "Hold your fire and don't hit Lane, for God's sake," he told the others joining him.

"Is he all right?" Mary asked.

"So far," Slocum said, knowing it was no use to tell her to get back. "He has a good lead and he's riding my good horse."

The sounds of the breeds screaming began to carry on the wind. Then came the pop of their pistols. Slocum could see puffs of smoke, but the odds of hitting anything from horseback were slim. Lane and the dun went out of sight in a dip.

They all held their breath. Then Lane came into view urging the dun on. He was close enough that the sound of the game pony's hard breathing and the creak of saddle leather was mixed with the pounding of his hooves.

"Get ready, boys. When they get up in full view, shoot and shoot straight," Slocum said.

Their rifles all popped at the same time. The screams of the breeds and their animals caught in the hot shield of lead carried above the wind. Lane was off the dun in a flash, with his Winchester sending round after round into them. The crew rushed forward, taking scattered shots and ending the breeds' attack.

"Is he all right?" Mary asked, holding onto Slocum's elbow.

"Yes, he's fine. The fight is over."

"Is he coming?" she asked, holding his arm.

"He's with the others, checking on the fallen breeds."

"Take me to him."

"Watch your step. There's lots of sagebrush here."

"I'll be okay."

"I didn't want you to fall down is all."

Her hand tightened on his arm. "Thank you, Slocum, you are a good man." She clasped her hands over his arm. "You have done so much for me."

He glanced over at her. Under the sunbonnet, she held her small red-rimmed eyes shut tight. Her chin raised, she went forward under his guidance.

24

There was no sign of Bobby Devereau's body. Slocum felt disappointed the leader had managed to survive. He glanced to the southwest. Devereau was still out there somewhere, and he would certainly cause more trouble before this drive was over.

One dead breed and one wounded. Counting the sniper, that made three fewer enemies in Slocum's book. Lane destroyed a dying horse with a pistol shot, and they hauled the slightly injured breed, who had been pinned under his horse, back to camp with them. Cartey was his name, and he wouldn't say much about Devereau or how many breeds there were left.

"Did the army find your camp?" Slocum growled at Cartey.

Seated on the ground, the buck scowled and acted deaf.

Filled with fury, Slocum grasped a fistful of his shirt, jerked the man to his knees, and drew his face close to his own. "You start talking now or I'm putting a rope around your neck and dragging you to your death."

"Army—come, burn some lodges—go away."

Slocum released his hold, and the breed grabbed for his obviously sore arm.

"Dugan, tie him up." Slocum felt discouraged the army hadn't done anything more than that. At last he spoke out. "I figure Devereau's still got more men than we have. But Lane, you did good."

Everyone agreed, and clapped the man on the back and told him so. Lane was the hero of the day. While they ate, he told everyone his story, about how he knew he could get the guard and the Sharps rifle before the rest of the breeds could get mounted and ride up the hill to the sniper's location. Only then had he wondered how much was left in the dun horse.

"Heck, you had them by a good lead," Luther said.

"When I came up from under that hill and saw your faces and rifles, it sure did make me feel good. Garnett, you ready to torture that breed into talking?" Lane chided the poor boy, sitting with his plate in his lap and his head down.

"I heard them Injuns would eat you." The cross-eyed boy looked ready to run away.

"Naw," Lane said. "You've got to eat *him*. How long is it going to take you to eat him?"

"A damn long time if I'm the only one eating on him," Garnett said with obvious dread, and drew more laughs.

"We still need two guards to the shift and don't be lax," Slocum said. "And Garnett, don't you shoot any more pole-cats on guard duty either tonight. It's hard to sleep when you kill them that close to camp."

"I thought it was an Injun sneaking up and I hollered at it to stop."

"Skunks don't understand damn English," Mark said, going to refill his plate.

"I'd shoot it again if it kept a-coming at me."

"Oh, boys, let's hope it don't have a mate," Blair moaned.

Slocum shook his head. Camp life was about back to normal. He looked at the red sunset. The cattle should be there in the morning. Mary came around with the coffeepot. He filled his cup and thanked her. Then, savoring the richness, he began to sip. Where was Snow Bear?

Then he thought of White Swan and what she was doing at Wounded Knee. She had been in the back of his mind since he left her. But it would never work out for him to stay with her. His presence would sooner or later cause her band more trouble, and might even have gotten some innocent person hurt already.

He found his bedroll early, and slept until they woke him for guard duty.

"How's it going?" he asked Dugan.

"Wolves howled a little early. Figure they're eating on those three dead horses out there," he said. "Nothing else."

"Thanks." Slocum took his shift riding around the horse herd, and was grateful when Lane replaced him so he could go back in his covers as the night cooled to chilly in the early morning hours. He speculated on what Devereau planned next for them. Slocum listened to the night wind—nothing. In a few minutes, he was back asleep.

The train came chugging out of the east with ten cattle cars. It halted in a screech of steel on steel, and prepared to back into the siding. The blue-uniformed conductor came from the caboose with his manifest and his shoulder to the wind to save his billed blue cap from blowing off clear to Alberta.

"You Lucas?" he demanded of Slocum.

"I'm Lucas's man."

"Got any proof?"

"I'm here, ain't I?"

"Yeah." The man threw his arm over his head to keep his cap on in the wind. "But you could be a rustler too."

"I could be Saint Nick too, but I'm not."

"Sign here. Guess you're official enough."

Slocum finished signing his name, and the conductor nodded in approval at it. "They're all yours, mister."

"Let's get them unloaded, boys," Slocum said.

The first doors slid open and the cattle came clambering out of the cars. Their horns had been tipped, Slocum noticed. The blacks, brindles, and some pinto-colored steers soon filled the pens and milled around. The cattles' hoarse bawling and the dust in the air soon filled the pens.

Mary's mules were hitched to the wagon, and within an hour, Slocum was ready to turn the cattle out. He searched for a possible lead animal, but the churned-up dust, along with the butting and fighting, made no single animal an obvious leader.

For the first day's drive, he chose Lane and himself as point riders. Slocum wanted to find a lead animal. Perhaps if they were lucky, they could bell him if he was good enough, and use him to save lots of cowboying to shape up the herd each time they were ready to move them.

The conductor came to find Slocum when the last car was emptied.

"That's all of them," he said, and Slocum nodded. He hoped that his counter, Luther, had the head count down correctly. He had assigned the boy to do that as the animals came off the cars.

The brakeman was standing beside the switch. Slocum nodded to the conductor. "You can tell Lucas in Billings we've started south with them, but that we've got some bad company. Devereau and his breeds are out there." Slocum tossed his head toward the south.

"Giving you trouble?" the conductor asked, holding on to his cap.

"Yeah, and I've got a wounded prisoner for you to take with you."

"Huh?"

"Turn him over to the military, he's their problem. Dugan! Load that breed on the train."

The man jerked the tied-up breed to his feet and shoved him toward the caboose. The conductor shook his head in disapproval, then bent over in the wind and followed them.

The prisoner loaded, Slocum went to find Luther.

"How many we got?" he asked.

"Eight hundred and twelve head."

"Good," Slocum said over their loud bawling. "I didn't see hardly any cripples, did you?"

"No, sir."

"The lame ones will show up soon enough. Get everyone mounted and we'll head them south. Tell Mary to follow us with the wagon." Slocum felt good about the shipment. On the whole, the cattle carried good flesh for longhorns, and looked healthy enough.

The first steers spilled out of the gate, and obviously were hungry, for they began to graze. That wasn't what Slocum planned, and he was forced to wave his lariat and shout at them to get their heads up. He was pleased to see that they acted tame. He drove the dun in close and choused the first ones toward the tracks.

It was a task to get them to cross the rails, and only persistent shouting and driving finally managed to send the first over, and the trek began. Some of the animals jumped the ties and tracks. Others were reluctantly forced over by the ones pushing from behind.

At the head of the herd, riding right point, Slocum rose in the stirrups, looking apprehensively over the herd and hoping that his riders in back had been able to drive all of the steers over the rails. He spotted Mary and Garnett bringing the mules and chuck wagon up wide of the herd. Lane was riding point with Slocum the first day, maybe not the best choice of jobs for the man. Mark, riding drag, might have the experience of his lifetime. Luther was bringing the horses. Slocum had faith in the youngsters and the farmers at each side, but it wasn't like riding with experienced drovers. The six of them would have their hands full simply moving the herd the next two weeks—without any interference from Devereau's breeds.

They reached the stream, as he'd planned, in mid-afternoon. Slocum lined the cattle out the best he could, using a big black steer as the leader, and spread them out all along the watercourse so they didn't butt each other into the water. The longhorns were thirsty, and that made him feel better. With their bellies full of water, they would settle down a lot.

With a wave of approval to Lane, who sat his horse on the rise above the stream, Slocum short-loped the dun to check on his other riders.

"Went good, didn't it?" Dugan asked, and Slocum nodded, seeing the last of the herd was filing down to the stream.

Slocum drew the hard-breathing dun in, and Mark and Luther rode over. The multicolored remuda was grazing placidly by itself.

"We have a few limpers," Mark said.

"Cut out the worst one to butcher later on this evening. We'll eat him," Slocum said.

"That ain't no problem," Mark said.

Slocum rode over to where Mary waited.

"Should we cross the creek?" she asked.

"Yes. We have plenty of time to set up, but we better let Lane drive the wagon over there for you."

Mary made a face, but then she nodded. "Shucks, Slocum, me and Garnett's getting good at driving these long-eared critters."

"I still want Lane to drive them over there."

"Land sakes, why, he thinks we're sissies, Garnett." She elbowed the cross-eyed boy on the seat beside her, and they both laughed.

Slocum was grateful when her husband rode over and took on the chore. Soon the wagon and camp were set up across the creek. Satisfied the steers had drunk their fill, Slocum and the others drove them through the water and up the other side. When the steers were scattered out at last across the rolling land and busy chomping on the grass, he decided to ride south and see the country they had to cover the next day.

Slocum chose a stout bald-faced horse from the remuda, and switched his saddle to him. He liked geldings better than these cranky studs from the breeds, but this animal was hard-muscled and looked powerful enough to carry him to hell and back. He swung up, holding the cheek strap on the bridle. When he gave the stallion his head, he took several stiff-legged bucks before Slocum managed to reel his head up, put spurs to him, and ride south in a long trot.

Where were those breeds? On a high point he reined up and used his telescope to scan the country. Nothing but a sea of waving grass. He wondered how far they would have to push to find more water. There should be enough moon lakes. He shrugged. No more smoke signals he could detect. But where was Snow Bear? Had the old man found the Spirit Woman, or had she found him? Slocum grinned to himself, recalling how the medicine man had discovered in Deadwood that women were all made the same. He liked the older Sioux and hoped nothing had happened to him.

He would play the drive south by ear. Short-handed as he was, it left him without anyone to spare to scout the way. Wounded Knee was in that direction, and he'd just have to correct his course as he went.

He turned the bald-faced pony back in the direction of the herd. It might take some real celestial help to ever pull this drive off. Above the wind, some taunting magpies scolded him as he sent Baldy northward.

25

Slocum stood in the predawn studying the first small purple streak on the horizon. The tin cup of steaming coffee warmed his hands. There was not much sleep for anyone taking turns riding around the herd. Mark was rounding up the remuda, and the damn stallions were screaming and kicking one another. Someone needed to take a good jackknife to the whole bunch of them. Then Slocum recalled the impatient angry Sioux women doing that to the dogs. Was he that mad about moving the herd? No, he simply wanted the second day to go well.

"Hear that?" Mary asked him, bent over and stirring her skillet of potatoes.

"Hear what?" he asked.

"One of those studs got out of the bunch and is across the creek back there. I heard him whistle."

"No," he said, considering her words. "Garnett! Get everyone up and armed! That's not one of our stallions over there! That's the breeds coming!"

"What?" she asked.

"Garnett, move! We haven't got time to waste! Mary, break out the ammunition! I've got to go and warn Mark and the others with the herd!"

He tossed the cup aside with a clink and hurried down the ridgeline to find the boy and their horses. He couldn't make out a thing except for the horizon to the north and the silver reflection of the water at the base of the slope.

"Mark! Mark!" he shouted.

"What?" the boy asked, coming up leading his horse.

"Ride out and get the two on guard in. Those breeds are about to attack the camp."

"What if they take the cattle?"

"Let them have the cattle. Get everyone back to camp. Their lives are worth more than two herds of cattle."

The youth bounded on his horse, and was gone in a thunder of hooves. Slocum hoped he had done the right thing, and hurried back to camp. Dugan was belly-down under the wagon with a rifle, Luther busy reloading a cap-and-ball pistol. Lane, Blair, and Mark came flying into camp on horseback, to Slocum's relief, when the first light of dawn appeared.

The breeds on horseback came screaming down the far creek bank. Slocum jerked up the Winchester and met their charge with a hail of bullets, and the others joined in.

The tide was turned, and while two breeds were shot off their horses, the others raced away on horseback. They soon reassembled on the ridge. Slocum and his crew used the wagon for cover and waited.

"We did good," Slocum said down the line to the others. "They don't like hot fire."

"What'll they do next?" Lane asked.

"Try us again. They're getting fortified up there." Slocum noticed them passing a crock jug around.

"How far will this shotgun shoot?" Garnett asked.

"When they get in the water, let loose," Lane told him, and everyone laughed. Mary went along behind them and issued ammunition.

"Get me that Sharps," Lane said to her. "I plumb forgot I got that."

She hurried to the front of the wagon, climbed on the wheel, and soon returned with the buffalo gun and cartridges. Lane used a lard pail for a tripod. Slocum watched him toss up some grass so he could test the wind. Then Lane flipped up the rear sight.

The long gun roared and a breed went sprawling off his horse. The others, with shocked looks, quickly reined their horses around and went over the rise.

"That wasn't such a damn good idea," Lane said with a shake of his head. "Now we can't see where they are or what they're doing."

"Least they ain't showing their bare butts at us," Dugan said.

Flies buzzed after Slocum. There was no sign of the breeds' activity, except when one occasionally stuck his head over and checked on them.

"They're having a war dance over there," Mary said, squatting beside Slocum. "I can hear 'em."

He trusted her hearing, and considered it might be some time before the breeds tried their next move. "Feed everyone. This may go on for a while."

"Good," she said, pleased, and called for Garnett to come and help her.

"Lucky we killed that beef last night. This may be a long wait," Lane said to Slocum as he sat up under the wagon with the Sharps across his lap.

"Could be," Slocum said, rising onto his knees. He had no idea how long the breeds would stay out there and what they'd try next. If he had enough manpower, he might try to charge and drive them off. But that wouldn't be the solution, because Devereau easily had three to his one.

"Slocum! They're getting our horses!" Mark shouted, pointing to the east. Downstream, several riders were driving off the remuda. Except for the three horses the night guards had ridden in on, Slocum and his crew would soon be on foot. Damn, nothing they could do about that. Devereau's bunch would cut them down in the open if they even tried.

"Hobble the others," he said, and the men rushed to catch the remaining horses.

They took turns eating breakfast and being on the lookout until the sun was well up in the sky. They remained close to the wagon, the food sitting heavy in Slocum's gut. He was responsible for seven other lives, and things looked bleak.

Then he heard war cries and the drumming of horses. They

were taking the cattle too. He had wondered if they would rustle the entire herd, or simply slaughter several for their own use, but obviously they were taking the entire herd.

"Can we stop them?" Lane asked, looking upset at the idea of the theft.

"Ride double maybe." Slocum shook his head in defeat. It would be hard to tell Lucas that Devereau's breeds had gotten the whole herd. It would be a real financial setback for the man. Slocum wondered if the military would pay reparations for the herd. They might have to lie and say the wild Sioux had taken them. Poor Lucas would be at least five years getting his money back, or those bankers' money anyway.

"What do we do next?" Lane asked, full of pent-up anger.

"See if we can hitch those saddle horses up and pull this wagon. I hope we can find an army unit to go after them. They were scouting all over the reservation."

"I hate that," Lane said, and the others nodded glumly.

"Breaking them horses to pull the wagon?" Slocum blinked in confusion at the crew.

"No, that those damn breeds stole the herd and the horses and mules too."

"Kind of like crying over spilled milk now. It won't do no good. Let's get this harness on them ponies."

The collar had to be padded with blanket material, and soon the harness was shortened and made to fit the tail-switching ponies. Slocum put his saddle on the paint left, and they loaded the wagon.

"We better walk," Lane said to the others when they were ready to move on. "Them horses will soon tire hauling this big wagon alone."

Slocum agreed with a nod, and he started ahead on the paint. At the top of the hill, he saw a distant line of riders, a war party. Hellfire, more trouble. He better get the others back to the stream so they had water during the siege. From the war bonnets, feathers, and bare brown skin shining in the sun, Slocum figured, there were perhaps thirty warriors. He sighed and looked to the heavens for help. *Why me, Lord?*

He loped the paint downhill waving for the others to all go

back. "A war party's coming!" he shouted over the wind. There was no end to his problems.

"How many?" Lane asked, using his hand to shade his eyes to see better.

"Three dozen or so," Slocum said, getting off his horse and joining the others. "We better fort up at the creek where we'll have water and some cover from the stream."

"It was a good plan, except we didn't find the army, did we?" Mary asked from the seat while she worked the reins on the ponies.

Slocum turned back. He couldn't see the Indians for the ridge. Then he shook his head. If he had any luck at all, it would surely be bad.

26

"Who is that?" Lane asked from beside Slocum where the entire crew lay under the wagon with their weapons ready.

Slocum opened his brass telescope and looked through the eyepiece. He blinked and stared through it again.

"Hold your fire," Slocum said. "That's Snow Bear."

"What's he doing heading a damn war party?" Lane asked.

"Be damned if I know, but I'm going out and find out," Slocum said, seeing the warriors on the hill forming a long line. He crawled out, told the others to stay put, and went to meet the medicine man, who was coming down the slope. The closer he drew to the man, the more he could read the glum look on Snow Bear's wrinkled face.

"Got here too damn late," Snow Bear said with a scowl, and reined up his horse.

"What are you doing with that war party?" Slocum asked, squinting against the bright midday sun to make out the other Indians.

"Damn, for two days I made smoke signals for them to come and help you."

"We seen the smoke and thought it meant trouble."

Snow Bear shook his head. "They didn't see it, so I had to ride down there, get them, and now I come too late."

"No. Devereau can't be far with the cattle. But we need some horses."

173

"How many horses?" Kicking Dog asked, riding off the slope with his great war bonnet fluttering in the wind.

"The ones that Devereau stole from us would be enough," Slocum said, greeting the chief.

"We will go get them."

"Good enough. I've got a horse to ride. I'll go with you." Kicking Dog grinned. "Them bucks up there can't wait for some fun. Don't be long."

"I won't," Slocum said, and started down the hillside on his boot heels. Damned crazy old medicine man anyway.

"What's happening?" Lane asked with an edge of uneasiness when Slocum reached the wagon.

"Stay put. Snow Bear and Kicking Dog's come to our rescue. I'm going with them after Devereau, the horses, and the herd. We'll be back for all of you."

"Well, I'll be damned!" Lane said, and scratched the top of his head. "We'll be here waiting, I guess."

Slocum nodded, and swung in the saddle with a wave to them. He sent the paint up the hill, and soon joined the yipping Sioux. They were ready for war. From their faces to their mounts, they had applied plenty of war paint. With rifles and lances, they galloped away to the south. Slocum kept up with them on the paint.

In less than an hour, he could see the herd's dust. Kicking Dog sent some of his men to the right and others to the left. The chief, Snow Bear, and Slocum, with six bucks, came up from the rear.

Slocum could hear the war cries ahead before his party topped the ridge. The fight was on. They pressed their ponies harder to reach the summit. He could see the sweeping charge of the warriors from the left. There was a short exchange of gunfire between the Sioux flankers and the breeds. Then the rustlers saw Kicking Dog and his men on the high point, and tore off to the west.

Slocum noticed the bug-eyed mules in the scattered horse herd. He had to make sure they did not get away in the confusion.

Kicking Dog and his men charged off after the retreating breeds. Slocum shouted to Snow Bear, "Get my mules!"

Snow Bear nodded. They both set out to capture the high-headed animals. Slocum loosened his lariat as his horse swept downhill. Uncertain if the paint would understand a rope whizzing over his ears, he held the loop ready and pressed him forward. The distance soon shortened between him and the two loping mules.

The rope swung over Slocum's head. Then he threw it, and the loop settled on the left mule's neck. He jerked the slack, took a wrap around the horn, and turned the paint off to the side, hoping the jerk wouldn't bring down his mount. The mule hit the end and the rope went taut. The saddle creaked, but the cinch and pony held, though it brought the charging paint to a sudden stop. Meanwhile, Snow Bear drove the other mule back to him.

Slocum nodded in approval. He stepped off and captured the second mule. Quickly, he fashioned a halter on him too.

"Them breeds don't want to fight," Snow Bear said in disgust, looking in the direction where the Sioux and the breeds had disappeared. "All run away."

"Looks like it. I need to gather them horses and get back so the boys can get these cattle herded up." Slocum looked in disgust at the scattered steers. "We'll be two days putting the herd together."

Snow Bear shook his head as if to dismiss his concern. "Sioux can do that for you."

Slocum looked at the man and grinned. "You're pretty good company to keep. You ever find the Spirit Woman?"

"No."

"Sorry I asked."

"I will find her."

"I don't doubt it. You know them smoke signals of yours like to have drove me crazy."

"Hmm," Snow Bear grunted. "You only one who saw them. You take mules. I will get those horses and cows in a herd."

"Steers," Slocum said to correct him. "They'll never have calves." Then he laughed.

Three hours later, with Mary's mules towing the wagon, Slocum on the paint, the two boys riding saddle horses, and the rest of his crew in the wagon with her, they all pulled up in sight of the longhorns. Slocum could hardly believe his eyes. All the cattle were in a herd and bedded down.

Slocum rode ahead and nodded in approval at Kicking Dog. "Your men did great work. We better cut out a couple and have a feast."

"Good. The women and children are over the hill," the chief said.

Slocum nodded. "We'll have us a big feast tonight in my camp."

The remuda horses were back, his men were mounted again, and things were close to normal. Slocum assigned the night guard duty to the crew, and explained about the feast he planned with the Sioux. Mary joined them with the coffeepot.

"What are those Injuns doing?" she asked.

"Fixing to have a feast and a stomp."

"What is a stomp?"

"It's a dance, like folks square-dance back home. These Sioux stomp."

"Could I learn how to stomp?"

"I'll have Snow Bear show you how."

She smiled and nodded in approval. "I smell wood smoke. Where did they get wood?"

Slocum shook his head. "By damn magic. They can always find it when they need it."

"Maybe I could learn some things from them."

"Maybe, Mary," he said, looking for White Swan, but not seeing her among the workers busy butchering nearby at the Indians' new camp.

His instructions complete, Slocum went and found the dun in the horse herd. He caught him and changed his saddle to the Texas pony, then rode out to make a great circle and see if they had missed any stock.

It felt good to have the easy long gait of the dun beneath him again. There was no sign of any stray steers, so he loped the dun over another rise to see if any had strayed further.

He reined up at the sight of a single familiar tepee in a windswept swale. Three piebalds raised their heads up and nickered at the dun. In a moment, White Swan slipped outside the opening and swept her long hair back from her face. She was dressed in the snowy white leather of the elk, and the long fringe swirled around her in the strong afternoon wind. Only a few blue beads decorated the rich dress that clung seductively to her shapely body.

"I wondered if you would come," she said, looking up at him.

"I can't stay long," he said with regret. "I have cattle to deliver, men to look after, a big feast." But he dismounted, and kept walking toward her as if drawn like iron dust to a powerful magnet.

They melted in each other's arms. His hat fell off, and she looked at him concerned.

"I'll find it later," he said, and they went inside the tepee.

On the buffalo robes of her lodge floor, they found the fire of passion rekindled into an inferno. Desire and need consumed them. In a flash they stripped their clothing away to bare their flesh. Muscles opposing muscles, their skin rubbed together like two fire sticks, until the friction sent the sparks into tinder and the fire burst forth in a blaze that consumed them. Finally, his brain swirled in the wildest stage of madness, he exploded, and it sent both of them falling into a heap of spent fury.

Slocum lay on his back, out of wind. The air rasped through his windpipe, and his eyes were dazzled by the dizziness. He wasn't on earth but somewhere else, transported to another world where the wind whistled through the rippling prairie grass and sang in the smoke hole of her tepee's crown.

This wasn't White Swan or Betty, the Cheyenne girl taught by the missionaries and once married to a Sioux warrior, the woman Slocum had made love with. Then a chill went through his body. Gooseflesh formed on his arms and he hurriedly dressed, realizing she had gone outside.

He rushed out the opening into the wind, combing his hair back with his fingers to look for her. Strangely enough, his hat lay flat on the ground only a few feet from where it had fallen off his head. As he searched for sight of her, he replaced the Stetson on his head. The black and white piebalds were gone, but his dun looked up at him from his grazing through the bits. Where was she?

Slocum rubbed the end of his dun's nose on the side of his hand. She was nowhere to be seen. Had he had a dream? No, his experience had been too real. He stuck his head back inside the tepee. Empty. The force of the wind tested the walls. It was as if no one had been inside there for a long time. No scents, nothing.

Disturbed and unsettled, Slocum went to the dun, gathered the reins, tightened the cinch, and mounted up, still dismayed by her disappearance. He blinked his eyes and looked at the sun setting over the far-away Black Hills. Maybe Snow Bear could explain it.

Later that night at the feast, he sat on a robe and watched Mary stomp with the Sioux women. The laughter rolled from the mouth of the small woman who, with her hands on the hips of her guide, stomped away.

"You eating?" Snow Bear asked Slocum with a grunt, seeing no food around him.

"No. I had an experience today," he began. "Out there."

Snow Bear nodded and hesitated, taking a bite of juicy meat from the rib in his hand.

"I thought it was White Swan and her tepee. It looked like White Swan, but she wore a snow-white elk-skin dress."

Bear nodded. "White Swan is at Wounded Knee."

Slocum decided his tale was too far-fetched to continue. He rubbed his hand over the beard stubble around his mouth. Who was the woman? Was he losing his mind?

Slocum glanced over at Snow Bear, who was nodding his head in approval and chewing a mouthful of beef. The juices of the meat were running in a small trickle from the corner of his mouth.

He waved the rib bone at Slocum. "Now I know she is out here!" Then his eyes twinkled, as if pleased with the knowledge.

"Who's out here?" Slocum frowned at him.

"The Great Spirit Woman."

Slocum narrowed his eyes at the man. A great knot formed

in his empty stomach. That was the spirit that Snow Bear had sought in the Black Hills. Why had she come to *him*? Things grew deeper and deeper. He wanted his head to clear, for all this to go away. He still had cattle to drive.

27

"Ain't bad," Lucas bragged. "Only ten head short and we're getting good weights on them."

Slocum scowled at the cattle buyer's back with displeasure as they stood in the sunshine near the Wounded Knee Agency building. Hell, Lucas had missed all the *fun*. The last bunch of steers were being individually weighed on the new scales. Several Sioux men were helping his crew do the work of poking the cattle up the chutes. Slocum felt his job was about over.

"You owe me two hundred bucks, plus when you pay off the crew, give Lane and his wife Mary those mules," he said.

"Huh?" Lucas blinked at him. "Why?"

" 'Cause you made so much money on this deal. Plus you and your partners are going to need a full-time crew to drive more steers down here. Lane and his bunch can do that. Oh, they'll need a couple more hands to help them, but they'll find them. May make cowboys out of some these Sioux."

"Our deal was only a hundred and fifty."

"Two hundred. I've had more expenses than I figured."

"Expenses? Where are you going anyway?"

Slocum shook his head. "No telling."

"Two hundred." Lucas shook his head in disgust at the amount. "I'll pay it, but you're robbing me."

"Good," Slocum said, looking over the crowd of Indian

women around the pens who were watching the weighing and waiting for their beef allotments. No sign of White Swan. Was she avoiding him? It was all right. He understood her feelings. Snow Bear could give her the money.

Lucas drew out a leather pouch from his pocket. "Suppose you're in a damn hurry to leave?"

"Yes, and you treat Lane right. I told him what to expect and about the mules—"

"How did you know I'd agree to that?" Lucas blustered, counting out twenty ten-dollar gold pieces into Slocum's hand. The coins glistened in the sunlight.

"I knew you would," Slocum said, and grinned at the man. His fist closed on the coins. Then he winked confidentially at Lucas. "Don't get too much of that Chinese stuff."

"Come by Billings sometime, I'll find you one. They're wonderful," Lucas shouted after him.

Slocum nodded, and stepped aboard the dun. He touched his hat and pushed the dun up the valley for Snow Bear's lodge. Earlier he had said his good-byes to Lane and the crew and kissed Mary on the cheek, and she had nodded yes to him in a most private way. Everyone was grateful when he shook their hands. He complimented each of them on a job well done. They knew about the deal he planned to spring on Lucas, and were excited about making the future drives.

"Come back and show us how to do it better sometime," Lane said when they parted.

Slocum dismounted heavily at Snow Bear's lodge. He dropped his reins to ground-tie the dun, then removed his hat and combed his fingers through his hair. The familiar gray-streaked head appeared as Snow Bear came outside.

"You are leaving?"

Slocum nodded. "I have some money for White Swan. I want you to deliver it to her."

"Why me?"

"A brother would do that for another brother."

"But perhaps she wishes to see you again."

"No, it would be better this way." He drew out the kerchief from his pocket with fifteen of the coins tied up in a knot for her. She would need the money for her and her son in the times ahead.

"I will deliver it to her, brother. But I am worried for you on this journey you must take."

"I will be wary too then."

"Be wary, brother. I do not wish to hear of your death." He placed a hand on Slocum's shoulder. "You took me back to the sacred lands, and I know I would never have gone there if you had not taken me."

"You no longer wish to go there?"

"No, the Spirit Woman is here now. She came to you. She will come to me sometime, someday. My heart feels good for I know where she resides. She resides with her people again." Snow Bear smiled.

Slocum put the kerchief with the money in Snow Bear's palm and his copper fingers closed on it. They nodded without words, and Slocum turned, feeling torn apart inside as he left his friend. When he settled in the saddle, he saw Snow Bear's nod. Then he booted the dun south.

Beyond the White River and into Nebraska, he entered the sand hills. It grew late in the day when he rode up to a ranch-store. The low log building was dug into a hillside. He stood in the stirrups and searched the corrals, seeing some spent horses but nothing out of the ordinary. Feeling safe enough, he hitched the dun and stepped up on the porch. Out of habit, he adjusted the holster around his waist.

Strange no one had greeted him. Most places like this, someone usually came outside and gave the new arrival a friendly hello. "Get off and stay awhile," or some such.

He lifted the latchstring, pushed the board door inward, and let his eyes adjust to the lamp-lit dimness of the room. A bearded man behind the bar nodded to him. Something about how this big man's hands were splayed out on the rough sawn-board bar made Slocum think instantly, *It ain't right in here.*

That instant he heard, "You sum bitch!" and whirled to see the breed's face.

Slocum could see the hatred and rage in Devereau's glare. Slocum's hand jerked the Colt free. At the same time came the sound of the chair clattering as the breed surged to his feet with his gun in hand. An orange ring of fire from the muzzle made a deafening roar, but the bullet went wide. Then the Colt in Slocum's fist belched deliberate death and destruction. Clouds of sulphurous gun smoke stung his eyes as the second round's recoil caused his hand to buck again. Through the gray veil, Slocum watched the breed slam hard against the log wall. Then his gun hand dropped and he slumped downward, until finally he collapsed in a pile on his butt. His head pitched forward.

All Slocum could hear was the wind outside in the eaves. The loud whistling sound tore at the rafter ends and caused something loose to continuously slap the side of the building, like someone whipping a horse to make it go faster.

"You hit?" the storekeeper asked.

"No." Slocum shook his head, frozen in his tracks. "You have any whiskey?"

"Damn right," the man said, then began to cough on the thick gun smoke. "I'll get some cups and we'll go out on the porch. Damn, it's bad in here."

Slocum walked over. Devereau didn't move. With his boot toe, he kicked the fallen pistol and sent it skittering across the dirt floor. Satisfied, he holstered his own gun and followed the man outside. The first breath of fresh air recovered his drained strength.

"Devereau ever mention a woman being with him?" Slocum asked, gazing at the grassy hills.

"Yeah, he did. Said she left him."

He nodded. Good. That meant Felica wasn't around to stab him in the back.

"My name's Curly France," the big man said, and handed Slocum a cup of whiskey.

"Slocum's mine."

"You from around here?"

He looked across the rim of the tin cup and studied the tall waving grass. "Nope, just passing through."

JAKE LOGAN
TODAY'S HOTTEST ACTION WESTERN!